Andrew Jackson and the Young in Heart

A Romance for All Time

Wilbur Cross

iUniverse, Inc.
New York   Bloomington

iUniverse books may be ordered through booksellers or by contacting:

iUniverse
1663 Liberty Drive
Bloomington, IN 47403
www.iuniverse.com
1-800-Authors (1-800-288-4677)

ISBN: 978-1-4401-7720-0 (sc)
ISBN: 978-1-4401-7719-4 (ebook)

Printed in the United States of America

iUniverse rev. date: 01/12/2010

Author's Note:

Though facts blend into fiction and fiction into fact, this short work is fully intended to be a <u>novel</u> rather than fictionalized history. Many of the people were real, the events factual. But that is beside the point. The Young in Heart are those who really matter.

Ageless are those who still suppose

The rain brings petals to the rose,

Who tolerate the winter's fling

Knowing it will soon be spring;

Who see in dreams some lesson learned

And not dark signs of passion spurned.

What prompted them to be so clever?

They are the Young in Heart forever.

-- Annie-Belle Donelson

Chapter 1

I was impetuously in love with Andrew Jackson.

The year was 1789. He was 22. I was 16. He was like no other man in the territory of Tennessee. Or perhaps in the entire republic, from the shores of the Atlantic to the sinuous banks of the Mississippi.

He was a shagbark type of a man, not a Tennessean by birth, but a maverick from the Carolinas. No one had ever presumed to earmark him as handsome. Indeed, his features were so etched by the whiplash of frontier life that he had more lineaments in his profile than two or three of his contemporaries put together.

He was born to be a general, yet the military was too confining for his skills; bred to be a philosopher, yet with more energy than was traditional in the role; structured to be a pioneer, yet more polished than rough-sawn; schooled to be a lawyer, yet more accomplished dealing with broad patterns than with the details of warp and woof.

From my earliest glimpse of the man, I could envision him only in an office that encompassed far broader dimensions than those in our range of familiarity. So it was never an astonishment to me that the Presidency was the ultimate perspective. The Presidency? We barely knew in those days, when General George Washington himself was a novitiate in the Chair of State, what a "President" was or could be presumed to be. Yet I could see in this young Jackson (*after the smoke of my girlish infatuation had cleared enough for my mind to be rational!*) the spark of greatness necessary for such a defiant calling. I did not hesitate to state as much, even in those days when his age was against him and he appeared strident of voice, dissonant of opinion, and frequently exasperating to his elders.

"You know a dozen eligible young men to select from for marriage, any of whom would whoop at the chance to relish your favors. Why is your gleam directed at esquire Jackson? He is too untamed and volatile for you."

My mother was a conventional, apron-strings lady who likened the course of one's life to a woodland stream, pre-directed by the slant of the terrain and always contained by the predicated embankments on either side. I, taking the opposite cast of her opinions on most issues of the day, saw life as an open ocean, sometimes calm, sometimes storm-tossed, pulled one way by the currents and another way by the tides and a complex mingling of savage forces. I saw life as on course only part of the time, and the rest wandering beyond the charts.

My passionate opinions of Andrew Jackson were as real as the embers that glowed on our kitchen hearth. Yet I lacked the power of convincing my peers, much less my elders, that I could deliberate in a logical manner. I was, you see, a poetess, a being even more irrational and contradictory than a poet I was also accused of being a free-thinker, exuberantly exploring ideas that were not considered "nice" for a maiden of eligible age. Not a few parents banned their daughters from socializing with me, for I voiced positive feelings about many a subject that was "naughty," and not a few that were "bawdy."

To be in love with a conventional type of hero was out of my focus. To be enamored of a total nonconformist like Andrew Jackson -- that was as nourishing to my nature as honey is to a bee.

"I hope you are in good spirits, Mistress Donelson," said Andrew Jackson, holding me spellbound with those eyes that reflected the blue of the sky over the Cumberlands.

"My name is Annie-Belle," I replied with a pout on that day I fell in love with him.

"Of course, of course," he laughed, "you are 'Annie' for the Scottish mists that kissed your cheeks at birth.

'Belle' for the capricious Southern beauty reflected in your chestnut eyes.

Was he mocking me a little? I would stand up to his impudence. For I was determined not to be taken for an old maid whom he should respectfully address by family name. Perhaps he did not realize that I had not yet turned seventeen and would for several years enjoy an age span considered "desirable" for marriage.

My petulance was uncalled for. He was gracious thereafter as we sat on the veranda at the home of my mother, a second cousin of Andrew's. He had not laid eyes on me for a year, not since his move to Nashville in 1788. I had flowered in the interim. Or so I had been led to believe by my aunt, a prissy spinster. "Your dress is too revealing," she was constantly cautioning me. She also liked to remind me that I was "maturing ahead of your years."

Irked by this wearisome phrase, I shocked her one day by blurting, "Do you mean, Auntie, that men are slyly glancing at the fullness of my breasts?"

I hoped that Andrew Jackson would have as discerning an eye as my aunt. He did not. He always looked me flat in the eye when he spoke to me and did not permit his glance to wander elsewhere.

I had heard much about Andrew as a distant relative, a rather unpolished frontiersman from the mountains of

North Carolina who had trekked west to the Southwest Territory to test his skills in the court of law in the town of Nashville. Oh, we were not a city then, having been federated only eight years before Mr. Jackson's arrival. Yet we did boast homes of many descriptions along the Cumberland River, as well as two general stores, two taverns, and a thriving distillery. Oh yes, and the Court of Law, more august in name than in its architecture.

"I understand from my cousin, Rachel, that you have solicited no end of clients," I remarked, having been advised by more sophisticated young ladies than I was, that the way to a man's heart was through interest in his brain, "and that you frequent the court almost as regularly as the Judge."

I had never been inside the courtroom. Yet I could picture barrister Jackson as a provocative figure standing before the bench. He was tall and thin, like a Bluegrass hickory sapling, jaunty of limb and gaunt of face. Though he stood just under six feet, he seemed taller, for his most notable feature was his hair, which stood straight as a sheaf of wheat above his high forehead, as bristling and unbending as the head of a broom.

Even when he spoke to me (*nothing more than a young female relative, I fear*), his eyes flashed the lucid blue of the sky over the Great Smokies on a crisp fall day. And the fire in his heart was the kind that burns -- mischievously on a hearth fed with sundried splits of oak -- not steadily and concordantly, but noisily and prone to unexpected outbursts of flame.

"Rachel is right," he was saying as these impressions of him were flashing through my mind, "As a fledgling lawyer, I faced an exciting situation when I arrived in town twelve months ago and found lodging at the home of your other aunt, the Widow Donelson. The town was literally an encampment of debtors.

"It seems that several sorry fellows who owed money had found refuge from their creditors by banding together so they could harass any who attempted collection."

He paused and patted his beetling chin with his long, rangy fingers, as though reflecting on the favorable circumstances. "My appearance on the scene was the occasion for the tables to be turned. By representing the creditors, Miss Annie-Belle, I in effect united them for a counterattack. Why, bless me, within the first month alone, I was able to enforce writs against some 70 debtors, who thus were compelled, if sullenly, to pay visit to the court."

Andrew (*I called him that in my mind, if not with my voice*) had a sharp-boned face, with a shaft of jaw that commanded attention. Gaunt as he was -- he weighed barely 127 pounds -- he could draw himself together so that he seemed all, fiber and resilience, a formidable man to oppose, whether in a corporal or verbal action.

He could orate on occasion with a raw elegance, the kind that is bred from within more than through any formal tutelage in elocution. He had the tongue of a purebred, nurtured close to the soil and uncluttered by the verbiage and idiom of the more congested haunts of man. His voice lacked formal cultivation and was often piercing and distracting. Yet it was as icily clear as the rock-splashing ruckle of a Cumberland Mountain stream.

He gripped my imagination, even when recounting the mundane findings in a legal case. I sat enthralled, because his emotions were strong and taut, like the string of a Chickasaw hunting bow. When he expressed himself, you could hear the pinging and the singing and the snap of his inner feelings as he sent his words, like arrows, to their targets.

"I cannot but admire your accomplishments. Mr. Jackson," I said after he had told of court matters, "yet I have a question."

"Speak out," he replied, with his blue, penetrating eyes fixed on mine and sensing my hesitancy, "I am accustomed to answering questions -- and forthrightly."

"Was there not some personal danger in all this? Had I been in your boots, Sir, I should have thought twice about aggravating a band of ruffians who had heretofore avoided paying their debts."

"Hah, hah!" he snorted, more with exuberance than humor. "There was risk indeed. Yet that was but the sauce to the pudding. For I was never certain when words might be replaced by rocks, thrown back in my face.

"I was, of course, constantly reviled by these devilish fellows with all manner of insults. It was a certainty that if I passed their ranks on the way to court I would end up before the bar with mud on my breeches or a button ripped off my coattails. Yet I have to admit that I relished this baring of teeth and raising of claw for being a barrister is, on most occasions, a tedious way to earn a living."

"I recall one irascible defendant who scuttled out of court after losing to me. His very manner warned of trouble almost before the door had closed behind us. Sure enough, when I walked past him, he deliberately set his heel down on my toe as hard as he could. Almost without losing stride, I snatched a loose picket from the courtyard fence and knocked him out cold. It was one of my most convincing points of legal procedure."

I saw Andrew Jackson quite frequently in those days for my mother's home was close to the big old house owned by my favorite aunt, the Widow Donelson, where the object of my undying love was boarding. Typically and Andrew was not reluctant to admit it -- he had selected this lodging because he saw that the Donelsons were one of the first families in Nashville and the association could do no harm to his emerging career.

My love for him, surging though it was at the start, continued to swell. Yet he was anything but the romantic hero a young lady might have pictured from the romantic narratives and ballads of the day. He often displayed a monumental temper, which he could hurl with righteous fury against his opponents. He frequently flooded public rooms with Anglo-Saxon expletives that brittled any one whose ears were not sheathed in iron. Still, the next moment he could be gentle and sentimental, tears blurring his eyes upon hearing about a local tragedy or the ill treatment of a child.

His nature was turbulent with these contrasting angular contradictions of manner, as well as opinion, so that it was not always easy for either his supporters or his opponents to understand on which side of an issue he stood.

"I think you are teasing me, Mr. Jackson," I complained to him one day when he had first spoken eloquently about the reasons why Tennessee should seek Statehood. When I agreed, he did a turnabout, peppering his own arguments with verbal buckshot. I ended up with the implication though I knew he did not really mean it that only a simpleton could imagine Tennessee as anything but a barbaric sprawl in the vast Southwest Territory.

"Statehood!" he erupted with such emotion that his straight hair bristled, "Nay. I had sooner invited the mosquito-infested swamps of the Mississippi Delta to join the Union than to annex this raw wilderness that mocks man's fruitless endeavors to civilize it."

Perhaps I with a nature that also tended to the contradictory and obdurate was intrigued by the contrasts that tempered the man. He could be impetuous, yet cautious; ruthless, yet compassionate; suspicious, yet confiding; condemning, yet loyal.

"Andrew, we are both from the same origins. We the lightning that terrifies the farmer far out in the pasture, yet strikes the dead stump in the swamp; like the thunder that simulates the noise of cliffs tumbling into a gorge, yet dissolves in the atmosphere. We must be kindred spirits."

I spoke this aloud far from his hearing -- for he would have laughed at my poetic nonsense as the outpourings of a giddy young maiden.

Indeed, I found myself trying to put the man into onomatopoeia as I relished his contradictions. With Scotch-Irish blood in his veins, he could display the worst of both cultures, and the best. He could harp endlessly on personal grievances -- then stand up for people who had defied him. He was civilized almost to the point of sophistication, maneuvering himself before a learned judge with all the magnificence of a frigate under full sail. Yet he was also a man of the forest, a frontiersman, risking a fragile canoe down the raging cataracts formed by the spring thaw.

Among my favorite accounts of his skills as a pioneer was the tale of Flint-Eye Morgan, a somewhat nondescript trapper who had accompanied him West from North Carolina to the Tennessee territory in 1788.

"Crossing the Appalachia," reminisced Morgan in his ragged idiom, "we was finding camp in a glen. Going to sleep I was. And the four othern. 'Cept Andrew. He's ta wake. Not a man for nodding.

"At midnight, he ketch the whoop of the owl. Agin, agin, agin, all around. Nex' I know, he is joggling my neck and clamping his hand to my mouth. "I think he's gone daft. 'Shhh,' he whispers, and 'Shhh. Injuns!' But I see no Injuns, hear no Injuns. No sounds but an owl. 'That's a savage!' he tells me, 'Let's go JL' "We wake t'othern and we run from that place like deer, Andrew aleading the way.

"Did you see any Indians?" I asked Andrew Jackson some weeks after hearing Flint-Eye's narrative. "The Devil no. They did not want to be seen. They did not expect that I would mark their voices either, disguised as the hoots of owls."

Then he placed his hand on my shoulder hard and poked that shaft of his jaw at me, almost belligerently. "I know what you are thinking," he chided, "that I concocted the story for a round of excitement."

"Well, how did you ever know that the 'owls' were Indians?" I asked, defensively, "Especially if you lit out of there fast and never saw any."

His grip relaxed and his eyes became moist. "I don't like to recall the ending," he said, rubbing his shagbark skin that had been scabbed by smallpox when he was 14, "for it saddens my spirit."

"The day after we had escaped, a party of hunters found our camp, the ground bedded and sheltered by a lean-to we had constructed. Grateful for the unexpected accommodations, they secured f or the night. They, too, heard the hoots of the owls in the surrounding forest, but interpreted them only as the natural voices of the woods."

"To make it short, the savages swooped in on them just before dawn and massacred them. All that is, save one hunter who had arisen early and gone to a stream to fetch water.

"If only I had left a warning sign the night before!"

He turned away from me, but not before I glimpsed the moisture running down one cheek.

"There in the forest lie the bones of our young men. Bones that might have been mine, to lie there bleaching and never destined to repose in a civilized place like Nashville."

"Ah, Annie-Belle, I am fortunate."

How I wished that his emotions any of them had been directed at me. It puzzled me at first that I did not arouse a more romantic response in Andrew. Though I was but 16 and he some six years older, I was so endowed in physique as to provoke sly glances from male strangers and undignified yawps from young men who knew me well. Moreover, I was articulate in the conversational arts and coquettish in the social graces.

"Why do you love him so?" I kept asking myself in the hope that it would assuage my passion to reflect upon his miserly physical endowments. As a boy, he had been as thin as a pipestem, and he still gave this impression of fragility, with his cadaverous mien, hollow cheeks, cragginess of profile.

"His appeal to women," explained my aunt, the Widow Donelson, one day, "is that of the infant to the mother, who senses the intuitive need to protect this mayfly in its helplessness."

Perhaps I was magnetized by more positive images. By the way he cocked his head slightly to the side when addressing me, so that he observed me with the side of his flint-blue eyes, rather than head on. This mannerism imbued me with the feeling that I were some one special.

Chapter 2

"Why in Heaven's name," said my mother one day with uncharacteristic exasperation "would that young man, Andrew Jackson, risk his career not to mention his reputation and probably brilliant future by going after Rachel?"

"He is contorting himself into the most unlucky, contradictory love affair, fraught with all kinds of legal, moral, and emotional complications. And I dare say serious risk to body and limb."

I felt quite the same way. But my voice carried little weight. Not only was my tender age against me, but I already had a "reputation." I came from Yankee stock, the suspect New Hampshire branch of the Donelson clan whose patriarchs were considered ill-educated and largely uncouth. Furthermore, at the age of 15 I had had the misfortune to play the role of an errant Cupid in the arrangement of an erotic liaison between the husband of an English gentlewoman and the wife of an absentee

Colonel in the militia. Since a small sum of money had exchanged hands, transported by me to the lady to pay for her journey to a trysting place, I exposed myself as a plump target for gossip.

"She is a bawd, pure and simple," proclaimed one of my maiden aunt's celibate female friends, "And with a suggestive name like Annie-Belle, I expect you will next hear that she has gone to work in a barroom.

Andrew Jackson had heard this tale of my lurid past and thought it all a roaring good joke. He considered elderly spinsters to be a brittle breed, whom he could shatter with the snap of his fingers -- which was fortunate in view of the highly unconventional course of romance that he charted for himself.

When Andrew Jackson migrated to Nashville he was 21. As he urged his horse along the dusty main street and then down by the river where he had been told the Widow Donelson's house was situated, he had no difficulty locating his objective. The house was, if anything, more substantial than he had been led to expect, two stories high, large enough to have held at any one time the mother and late father and all eleven children, plus several servants who occupied quarters in the rear.

The semi-Georgian house was close to town, framed by a grove of poplars and surrounded by pastureland on three sides and the river on the fourth. Andrew dismounted in the circular front driveway, hitched his horse to a stalwart oak post, and walked briskly up the planked steps to the wide veranda. The door was already open, in its habitual state of welcome. Before he had a chance to reach for the iron knocker, his boot steps on the hardwood timbers had already announced him and the Widow Donelson appeared on the threshold to greet him.

She was a plump, round-faced, talkative woman who radiated gregariousness and good humor.

"I knew ye straightaway, Andrew Jackson," she said in her homely voice, "Ye have yer mother's face and yer father's broomstick hair."

She swept him inside and would not permit him to un-sling his saddle pack and duffle from his mount until she had fortified him with a cup of strong Irish tea.

'Tis Armagh," she said as she handed him the steaming cup, "which your mother used to buy in Carrick-fergus before she left the Old Land."

"Thank you, Madam," replied Jackson politely and a bit timidly, for he was not yet as comfortable with social conversation as he was later to become. Whenever he could do so inconspicuously, his eyes swept around the parlor, assessing this new environment in which he himself had chosen to abide.

"If you don't mind," explained the Widow after they had finished tea and he had brought in his dusty luggage,

"I'll have one of my daughters, Rachel, show you up to your room. I have a carbuncle on my left foot and find it very hurtful when shinning the stairs."

She hallooed in the direction of the kitchen. He heard the instant sound of light feet pattering out. It was at that moment that Andrew Jackson *saw the vision*.

Rachel was a daughter of the South, a dark-haired, dark eyed beauty, petite and soft-limbed. Where Andrew was gaunt and spindly, she was full-complexioned and well curved; where he was loose-jointed and ruffled, she was firmly boned and composed; where he was chiseled by wilderness encounters, she reflected the grooming of the parlor.

Yet they shared a common spirit he an unquench-able thirst for action and she a constant vivaciousness, as befitted a lass with an Irish look about her and high spirits inside. She was a lively sprite who liked to dance, ride, and concoct the most preposterous tales.

I really did not know my cousin, Rachel, well, for she moved in completely different circles and at a higher level of society than I did. Besides, she was Andrew's age take three months and more likely to consort with grown-ups than with giddybrains. It was natural that she would appeal to a person of Andrew's temperament, for her personality was a calico of contrasts.

She could be as ladylike in the parlor as a dowager in a church pew. She also liked to smoke a pipe.

Andrew Jackson was in love with Rachel almost before they had reached the landing and he had caught a glimpse of her petticoat and delicate, bare ankles under her gingham skirt. She was to be his first love, his last love, his only love.

She was the first of the breed I came to know as the Young in Heart.

"This is your bed chamber, Mr. Jackson," she said softly, pointing to a smallish room with a large brass bed and an ample set of drawers, but otherwise sparsely furnished. "It is not, as you see, very elegant."

As she turned to leave him to the privacy of his unpacking, her voice crackled with an impish tone, "But don't you be expecting to pass much time here, except when in slumber. The kitchen and parlor are yours at all times along with our company."

She closed the door with a snap of her wrist and was gone.

For my young barrister from North Carolina, the next few evenings were a delight. When he returned from his diurnal chores in the cramped office he had engaged to share with a court solicitor, he found the Donelson household a whirl of activity. Amidst savory odors from the kitchen, promising a hearty repast, young people of both sexes and varying ages engaged themselves in whatever suited their fancy. An older daughter was always at her needle point, humming softly to the tunes of a flute in the hands of a younger brother. Another youth might be in the corner, romping, with proper restraint, with the family's Irish terrier, the only animal permitted inside the house.

As for the Widow Donelson herself, she was in and out of the parlor, often to summon a few minutes of help in the pantry.

Andrew relished the bustle around him, yet was hardly aware of who was doing what. For although he tried to be polite and disguise his partiality, he had eyes only for Rachel. When he was seated in the lumpy and brocaded guest chair near the fireplace and Rachel was completing a chore in the buttery, he felt as though he were separated from her by a mountain divide.

When she appeared in the doorway, removing her homespun apron as a sign that her chore was finished, it was as though the sun had burst through a dark cloud, a spring breeze had coursed through a dank vestibule, and lilacs had breathed their fragrance through an open window.

How she could exploit the mere fact of her presence! Her dark eyes caught the sparkle of life, like a black pond at midnight, suddenly rippled to catch moonbeams.

Her lips curled in a provocative little crook that meant mischief. Her eyebrows arched and her nose tip-tilted in a warning that she had some outrageous scheme in mind. Her chin dimpled ever so slightly, a sign that she was determined to fan a little flurry of excitement and wanted to be egged on.

On the very first evening after Andrew's arrival, Rachel suddenly enlivened the scene after having helped her mother whip fresh butter for the next morning's breakfast. In no time, she had not only the younger family members but her plump-waisted mother and the sober barrister from North Carolina contorted into the most preposterous poses.

"It is a quaint new game I learned from a Creole tinker," she had explained, pointing out that the object of the diversion was to see which players could balance the most buttons on their noses and chins at the same time.

"Why would a tinker ever be the one to suggest such sport?" asked the older sister.

"Ah-ha," replied Rachel, always one to appreciate an act of innocent guile, "he was a sly one. He sold me more buttons than I had intended to buy. And also a modest prize, which I shall bestow upon the winner."

On the second evening, Andrew considered himself most fortunate. Overhearing Rachel tell her mother that she was going to ride across the pasture to look for a lost lamb, he volunteered to accompany her "in case the animal may be injured and need to be carried back."

He was encouraged to note that his plea before the bench was not necessary.

"Oh, I shall be most happy with your company, esquire Jackson, whether we locate the lamb or no," she replied coquettishly. He half suspected that she had fully intended to be overheard. The idea that she wanted his companionship, without sharing it with her brothers and sisters, made his face flush a most uncommon condition indeed.

As it turned out, no lamb was found. Or even missing. The herdsman had simply miscounted as the sheep filed into the fold that afternoon and had reported the loss reluctantly after himself searching to no avail.

Andrew cantered off to work on the third morning of his stay, complimenting himself on his good fortune. Had he the voice for singing, he most surely would have startled passersby with an outpouring of melody. As it was, the court solicitor, who had stopped by his desk at the time Andrew arrived in order to gather some papers, wondered seriously whether his office-mate had been sampling the local bourbon. He did seem a bit giddy, especially for that hour of the morning.

That evening, Andrew Jackson received an abrupt, and certainly unexpected, shock. He learned that Rachel was married!

The revelation came about shortly after supper when the Nashville town courier knocked at the door, held up an epistle sealed and stamped in wax and inquired whether "a Mrs. Robards" was in residence.

"Oh, yes," replied the Widow Donelson who had risked aggravating her carbuncle to scurry to the door, "she is here and expecting word from her distant husband."

Jackson, expecting that it must be the oldest daughter she so constantly preoccupied with her needlepoint was dumbstruck when the Widow returned from the vestibule and promptly handed the envelope to Rachel.

It was fortunate that my favorite aunt, the Widow Donelson, was a discerning soul. For all her external conviviality, which sometimes gave her an air of superficiality, she was within a person of great insight. She sensed Andrew's reaction almost at the same instant that Rachel was opening the letter. Privately, during the course of the next few days, she imparted to him the facts about her daughter's marriage.

Some two years earlier, Rachel had married Lewis Robards, a Kentuckian of good family and had gone north with him to live in Kentucky.

"Captain Robards had a very suspicious nature," explained Mrs. Donelson, "and began accusing Rachel of all manner of improprieties, especially since he was away on military duty much of the time and she was left alone many a day and night.

"Oh, I cannot blame him completely. My daughter is ... well, coquettish. She cannot resist speaking with her eyes and dropping compliments. Not if it will result in equal flattery to herself. 'Tis the Irish in her, that and her Southern ways."

"Where is Captain Robards now?

"Him? Why in Kentucky still. You see, he ordered her out of his house. *Ordered* her! He did not like the friendly way she addressed one of his friends. Imagine! Why if he lived with me, an amiable sort, he would think I was a loose woman. If ye'll pardon my bluntness."

I would be damned were I to describe Andrew as an "opportunist." In truth, he was a more positive sort, a man who seized opportunity. Rachel's marital situation would have discouraged every other eligible bachelor in Nashville and did. Not so, Andrew Jackson. His reasoning went like this: Rachel was alone. Her husband, though distant, was perfectly capable of taking his wife back. Therefore, Rachel was unwanted. No young lady, especially one with beauty and wit, should remain unwanted. Wherefore, it was natural and desirable for a new suitor to enter the stage and convert a sad ending into a happy one.

Within two days, no more, Andrew had completely regained his composure. He was courting Rachel as actively as though she had never lain in the bridal bed. Rachel, for her part, was as merry as a schoolgirl, singing, telling lively tales, and enticing friends and relatives alike into all sorts of convivial games and diversions.

Had her mother permitted it, she might even have joined in the local dances.

Andrew was a happy man. As happy as a man in love might be who could live in the present and choke off his thoughts about the future. But an event took place a few weeks after the delivery of the fateful epistle that once more challenged his singular brand of determination.

Andrew had been at his office working on a court solicitation late into the night. The Donelson house was dark upon his return to it and he climbed the stairs to his chamber and went to bed. In the morning, he was surprised to find that, when he descended to the kitchen, Rachel was not at the stove, assisting her mother, as was her custom.

The Widow Donelson, moreover, was distraught and red-eyed. She most decidedly had been weeping. Was Rachel ill? Was something wrong?

"It's that dastardly Robards!" she exclaimed, her usually calm voice rattling as though she had a mouthful of pebbles.

"Robards, he arrived in his carriage last evening, just at suppertime. That was what the letter had been about -- his decision to take Rachel back. We did not think he would really come here. He changes his mind so quickly. Like a child who does not know what he wants."

"He is in town now?" asked Andrew, already trying to anticipate the next move and plan a decisive counter-action.

"No, no. I am thankful you two will not meet. We have already had a scene such as I could not survive a second time. My Rachel was in tears. Robards was insistent. He hauled her into his carriage, in the middle of the night, and headed back for Kentucky. By now, they probably have crossed the border."

"That's *abduction*!" bellowed Andrew Jackson, swearing a bloodcurdling oath that made the widow's cheeks turn pale and her heartbeat race. "Damnation! The man can be buckled into court, fined, and possibly put in irons!"

"But Rachel is *still* his wife," whimpered the widow, more distraught than ever. The captain told me it was the right of a husband, aye, the duty to keep the marriage in stew."

"In situ. In situ. A Latin term. It was that devil's manner of trying to make you think his action was legal. Well, we shall see about that."

Then, seeing that his display of emotion and temper was unsettling his beloved landlady, Andrew abruptly calmed himself and assured the widow that everything would work out for the best in the end. He would personally see to that.

"It isn't fit for fair," sobbed the widow, "This marriage was as sour as week-old milk from the start. The two are no more suited to one another than a hummingbird is to a jay."

I saw Andrew twice in the weeks that followed, when I had occasion to visit my aunt. He was in his 'gladiator' mood, itching for a fight. Only the fact that he had a responsibility to Rachel's mother prevented him from putting stirrup to steed and heading north across the fork of the Red River and into enemy territory, Kentucky.

How long this stalemate might have continued no one can guess. But then came the letter.

It was two months after Rachel had been snatched from the family hearth. The same town courier arrived at the Donelson home, this time in mid-afternoon, with an epistle for Mrs. Donelson. She did not read the contents to Andrew that evening -- the details were too intimate, the tone too emotional. However, she did impart the essence of the message.

"Rachel has reached the bourn," she reported sadly. "She can punish herself no longer and is ready to leave that savage. I must outfit my carriage and go to her at once."

"By no means," exclaimed Andrew, the scar on his forehead glowing like an ember and revealing the emotions deep within him, "It is *I* who shall undertake that journey. I have shilly-shallied too long already and allowed my convictions to become clouded with irresolution."

"Captain Robards will do *me* no harm," argued the Widow weakly, "but there is no telling what desperate assault he might make on your person. In his eyes, ye are an enemy, a cause of his predicament."

"I leave in two days," said Jackson firmly, as though my aunt had not spoken a word, "Tomorrow I enter postponements in my court cases. And the day after, I leave. That is my decision."

Chapter 3

Characteristically, Andrew Jackson declined the comforts and convenience of a carriage, caparisoned with blankets and rain gear and stocked with food and beverage. Instead, he rode horse-back, with the barest essentials, trailing a second mount for Rachel. If there was danger and a threat against life or limb, he was ready for that eventuality. Yet he did not mean to tarry and engage in any polemics with Robards.

"If the man challenges me to swordplay or pistols," he told his office mate, "I shall meet him forthwith on the field and have done with it. So much the better. But please do not convey this intention to the Widow Donelson. She would be unnecessarily disquieted.

"Such action is little likely to come about, for men like Robards cannot come to unwelcome decisions."

As it turned out, the trip to Kentucky to rescue Rachel was uneventful -- perhaps more so than Andrew had expected and hoped for. He saw not a sign of Captain

Robards, that unhappy personage having departed to Lexington for a three-day tour of military duty. Rachel was surprised, but ebulliently pleased, to see Jackson gallop early one morning up to the Robards cabin. Stuffing her meager personal belongings in a saddle bag, she was on her mount and accompanying her rescuer southward towards Nashville almost before the startled servants realized they had an unexpected visitor.

Winding their way along a trail by the Red River, Andrew and Rachel decided not to head for the settlement at Clarksville but to spend the night in a copse, well off the trail.

"Is there any danger of Indians?" Rachel asked, her voice tinted by more of a sense of adventure than trepidation.

"There is always that peril," laughed Andrew, already relishing his self-appointment as the champion and protector of a maiden in distress, "but I doubt that we would encounter even a renegade in these parts. Shawnee were reported here five or six years ago, but were forced West, past the Mississippi."

After they had made camp and unrolled their sleeping duffels on a bed of pine needles, Andrew displayed his talents as a cook by transforming dried venison jerky into a stew, to which he added wild onions and pepper grass for seasoning. He also produced a flask of Madeira, which he habitually carried on journeys as an internal antidote to stomach chills and an external antiseptic for insect stings.

"Why, Mr. Jackson, this is the most elegant banquet I have enjoyed in many months," said Rachel as they sat side by side in the rosy glow of their tiny fire.

"We have desert, too."

"What could that be?"

"Ramekins. They are tasty, and said to be an aid to digestion."

From an inside pocket in his jacket, he brought forth a leather pouch. In it, wrapped in thin parchment were several tiny cakes, moist and exuding the fragrance of fine Jamaican rum.

With the last drop of Madeira drained and the rumcakes consumed, Andrew Jackson and Rachel enjoyed each other's company in a blanket of silence, almost hypnotized by the capricious flickering of the embers and the muted whisperings .of the green forest that enfolded them on all sides.

Since my first wish, to have Andrew Jackson as my lover, was never to become true, my second wish would have been to be a wide-eyed, sharp-eared owl perched in the darkness above these two. Although the silence was deep, it was manifest that Andrew's mind was a tumble-tub of words and endearments -- all trying to spill out.

You see, this was another of these magnetic contradictions in his nature: He was an incurable romantic, churned inside by the most sentimental emotions. He was also an eloquent speaker who could thread his expressions through the eye of a needle. Yet when it came to avowing his own most intimate passions, his tongue became butter and he could not form the words. Thus it was as he sat in the forest beside his one and .only love, the night air redolent with his manliness and her femininity.

Rachel, habitually pert of tongue, seemed content beyond measure with this rare span of quietude. It was almost like kneeling before some darkened altar, soundless yet being spoken to by another being with a power beyond your own.

Finally Andrew Jackson coughed nervously. (*How I should have relished seeing him tongue-tied just once!*)

"Rachel ..." he began raspingly. Then, clearing his throat, "Rachel, there comes a time in the affairs of every man..."

"Why Mr. Andrew, are you going to practice an oration on me?"

He was silent. I can imagine that his sheaf of straight-rising hair bristled in a sign of indignation.

His countenance fell. "Damnation, girl! No I am not practicing an oration. I am about to inform you that emotions are stirring in my breast -- in my heart that you should know about. For they concern you. In truth, you have caused them."

He pounded on the front of his tunic. "I cannot dislodge them now, even knowing that you are married to another man."

Rachel's voice softened. She leaned against him and locked her hand against his elbow. "I know that, Andrew. I have known it for a long time. You have told me many times over, with your look, your eyes, your actions what is in your heart."

"Aye, Rachel. I guess I knew that. I was only afraid that if I did not express myself in words -- after all, that is the tool of my trade -- you would look upon me as no more than a warm friend."

She took his spindling hands in her small delicate ones and pressed them fondly to her lips. "Love is more in the spirit than in the voice. Let us get some sleep so we can be on our way early. By tomorrow nightfall we shall be back in Nashville. From there we can chart a course of action away from the shoals on which our love has been stranded."

For all their hopes, now united, the solution remained ever elusive. Captain Robards had taken it upon him self to be incommunicado. During the next few months, the Widow Donelson tried to reach him through a mutual friend who lived in Kentucky. Her hope was that he would relent -- seeing that the marriage was beyond repair -- and give Rachel her freedom.

"Divorce is a brittle word in my ear," said the widow dejectedly, "and 'twould make my dear, departed husband lie uneasy in his grave. Still, it is the only path to happiness for my daughter."

Although divorce came to be talked about openly in the inner circles of the Donelson family, no one knew better than Andrew Jackson how difficult and complicated the legal proceedings could be. Few solicitors were schooled in that body of the law. And frontier courts, overloaded with cases of a more violent nature, tended to be anything but obliging to the parties involved.

"We don't have time to coddle couples with emotional tantrums," said one judge bluntly, "Let 'em shoot it out and the undertaker take the spoils."

Whenever I visited my aunt's home during these trying circumstances, I could see why Rachel so magnetized Andrew. Throughout it all, she continued to be as puckish, mischievous, and wild-spirited as she ever had been. Her looks, her manner, her demeanor -- all encouraged him to keep ardently in pursuit.

The stalemate was shattered in the spring of 1791, almost three years after Andrew Jackson had trekked to Nashville and hitched his horse outside the Widow Donelson's home. The first hint that something was afoot came when the Widow's former hostler, a man of almost 70, galloped southward and into the compound. His horse was frothing and the poor rider so drenched in perspiration it was feared that he might have a heart collapse.

"I have ridden all day and part of the night," he panted, lying on the parlor couch, with the Widow patting his hands and arms to help keep the blood circulating.

"Do not exert yourself, I beg you," she pleaded, "Whatever you have to say can certainly wait ten minutes until you are able to draw breath more comfortably."

As it turned out, the poor man had been on a mission to Fort Boone to purchase some Kentucky thoroughbreds for his new employer when he had run into Captain Robards.

Robards, either fortified with bourbon or in an irrational state of mind, had chastised the elderly hostler without reason. Thinking him to be still in the employ of the Donelsons, he had given him dire instructions.

"Ride south as fast as that lard-shanked mare of yours will carry you. Tell my wandering wife, Rachel, that I am coming for her as soon as I finish my duties here at the post. And this time I expect to chain her like a bitch in heat so she cannot stray from my bed and board again.

"Oh, and also," he yawped ferociously, gripping the hostler's wrist so hard that the blood was crimped from it, "warn that would-be wife-stealer, Jackson, that I have just purchased a brace of new Cavalry pistols with fast hammers. I am anxious to see how quickly the balls will pierce his thick skin."

It was more than evident to the Widow Donelson that Rachel would have to go into hiding. But where? If she remained in, or near, Nashville, Captain Robards would surely smoke out her whereabouts. He had too many old cronies who, for small favors or a jug of spirits, would gladly play the bloodhound.

"How about Natchez," suggested the old hostler, "don't you have kin there?"

"To be sure," replied the widow, "a cousin-in-law who has been fond of Rachel and my oldest daughter since they were teething age. But that is a far, far piece."

"The farther the better, I should judge. I make it about 450 miles. But Rachel can travel part way along the Tennessee by riverboat, then down the Mississippi by barge. Much easier on the carcass than horseback."

By the time Andrew Jackson heard about the incident, the Widow had made up her mind. She and Rachel would depart within the week.

"I'll not let you do it," said Andrew resolutely, "We have to stand up to these savages in civilized clothing, or they will take us over and make us savages, too."

In the end, he gave in to the ladies, recognizing their fears, but only on one condition: that he, not the Widow Donelson, accompany Rachel to Natchez.

I knew how strongly Andrew felt about Rachel when he agreed to abet the escape, for it was entirely contrary to his nature to turn his back on any adversary or to avoid an issue head on. Once he had made his mind up, though, nothing could alter his decision.

Arguments against his going were as strong as those in favor of it. "Ye know," repeated the Widow several times over, "it is not fitting for a married lady to be accompanied by a single man -- an eligible bachelor -- without any sort of chaperone."

"Do not try to test my resolve," retaliated Andrew, "at least you will have the comfort of knowing that Robards will have no one to attack, with both Rachel and me out of sight and out of reach."

In view of later developments, I have a burning suspicion that Andrew might also have realized the potential of a clever feint. By accompanying Rachel he provided Robards with justification for instituting divorce proceedings -- something he did not previously have in his arsenal. He could claim infidelity, traveling unescorted with a member of the opposite sex, desertion, or living with a man other than her husband.

I could almost see his keen legal mind probing that of his distant rival, outguessing him -- like a crafty chess player getting inside the brain of his opponent to anticipate the moves he would make. There was indeed something prophetic in a remark he made about this time. When told that Robards had publicly proclaimed that he would never give up Rachel, Andrew interpreted this as a clear sign that he would do just the opposite.

"Now I know he's setting himself up to let his wife go. It's characteristic of his breed, a type given to vacillation and indecision. A sudden change of mind is his way of asserting himself."

The journey to Natchez took eight days. Andrew insisted on starting along the Tennessee in a leaky canoe, which he could later discard. They hiked part of the way to the great Mississippi and continued in relative comfort by barge to their destination. For Rachel, it was a rousing adventure, as she absorbed unfamiliar sights and heard unaccustomed sounds. The barge, overloaded with bales and rough-toned plainsmen who seemed to be speaking a different language, was never the less a stage on which she viewed ever-changing patterns. Most of the passengers seemed to be headed for the Gulf, talking endlessly about the wealth of fresh fish they could net in one haul, the succulence of wildfowl, almost too plump to fly from gorging on shellfish, beach crabs and other sea creatures, and the richness of the soil in the Delta, spewed there over centuries by the broad river.

"Corn grows so big," joked one gawky fellow from Arkansas, "a lubber must cart each ear by barrow, fer he kenna lift it."

The color and exuberance of the drift south was a mixed blessing for when the flat boatman finally eased his barge shoreward and announced that this port was Natchez, Rachel cast a gloomy eye at Andrew to make sure she was not being teased. It looked as though the Mississippi had sluiced all of the mud from the last hundred miles of bottom to this saucer and slopped it against the base of the high bluffs that commanded the river.

Natchez was still a Spanish settlement. There were a few elegant homes along the top of the bluffs, but most of the activity took place in what was referred to as Natchez-Under-the-Hill. The chocolate waters were alive with flatboats, barges, Indian canoes, long-pole rafts, and clumsy barges with smudgy sails. As the barge was poled towards a rickety pier, Rachel heard a mélange of dialects - Spanish, Creole, Indian, French, and she knew not what.

"Oh, Andrew," she said, looking up at him protectively, "will anyone be able to comprehend where we want to go?"

"I imagine we'll get to your aunt-in-law's ," he replied confidently, "once we find out where most of the residences are situated."

He drew forth the letter of introduction that the Widow Donelson had given him, and studied it to see whether it provided any directions.

There were no inscriptions on it, save the name and the script in the Widow's crabbed, almost illegible hand asking that "Rachel be provided with friendly refuge for a few weeks until a distressing circumstance has been resolved and she is at liberty to return home without peril to her person and effects."

It was almost two hours before the two dusty, mud-footed travelers succeeded in their quest and completed a very circuitous route to the home they were seeking. Their destination turned out to be a cabin set in cotton fields a mile to the east of the river. The cousin in-law, who had lost her husband two years earlier, was by no means as gregarious as the Widow Donelson. She had not laid eyes on Rachel since the latter was a girl of 14 or 15. Nevertheless, she was sympathetic and understanding.

She was particularly cordial to Andrew, and with reason -- as he shortly found out. Her only children were two daughters, 19 and 21, who had not found husbands and were not likely to in a land where there were few bachelors except for rough-tongued rivermen, itinerant trappers, and arrogant Spanish officers who were always looking for women, but not with marriage in mind.

The young ladies were shy and as plain as corn cakes. Yet a remarkable transformation took place. They were strangely captivated by this Quixotic Tennessean, who could be as loquacious and persuasive in a farmhouse scullery as in a court of law. In no time at all, they were laughing with him, parrying when he teased, and trading jest and stories with great animation. Eyes that had been dull crinkled with gaiety; lips that had been straight curled with levity; cheeks that had been wan flushed with vitality.

"Why that Mr. Jackson could turn a toadstool into a tulip," whispered the elated mother to Rachel after they had enjoyed a lively dinner at the kitchen table that first evening in Natchez.

It is no wonder that she and her daughters were dismayed when Andrew reckoned that he would be heading north in two days, once he could find and purchase a proper trail horse.

"It was my plan right along," he explained when the cousin-in-law tried to persuade him to remain. Having intuitively characterized him as a 'knight-errant, she had tried to take advantage of his benevolence by hinting that they would soon need a strong pair of arms to help with the cotton crop. The scheme did not succeed, for

Andrew was concerned about the pending court cases he had left unfinished in Nashville and was unswerving in his decision to return promptly.

"I shall follow the Natchez Trace," he replied, when asked what route he had selected for the return trip.

"Oh, but Mr. Jackson," exclaimed the elder daughter, "That is little more than an Indian trail along the hills. I understand that travelers are beset by savages, bandits, and cutthroats."

"True ," said Andrew in a matter-of-fact tone, glancing at her with his typical sideways cock of the eye, "In Nashville, we refer to the Trace as 'Satan's Spine,' Be that as it may, most of the bumptious fellows you speak of are renegades, deserters from the militia, and petty thieves. You have but to roar at them in a harsh voice and brandish a loaded pistol to make them dissolve into the thickets like dust from a horse' s hooves."

Andrew Jackson departed from Natchez as promptly as anticipated, leaving behind four moist-eyed females who were dejected to see him go. As for Rachel, it had been pre-arranged that she would await the arrival of two older brothers who were military scouts and could take leave of absence to fetch her, once Mrs. Donelson felt assured that Robards was no longer a threat.

It so happened that I was crossing the Nashville Common on the way from the market when Andrew's familiar figure passed by on horseback, mere hours after his reappearance in town.

"Mr. Jackson!" I called to him in delight. I was 18 by then, in the full blossom of womanhood, and hoping that he would give me more notice than he had the preceding year -- or even six months past.

"Why, Annie-Belle," he greeted me jovially, "mount up behind me and I'll trot you home."

"Oh no," I replied coyly, "I have in this basket eight eggs -- fresh and fragile -- and a tin of warm milk. I know you too well. You could not resist a gallop. I would end up with an uncooked omelet were I to accept your invitation."

"However," I added brazenly, "I should be happy to ride beside you of an evening, should you be seeking company in the freshness of the night air."

"So it shall be." he laughed heartily, though in a manner that left me doubtful that I should receive another invitation, day or night.

To tell truth, I was at that time content not to be any more closely involved. The strange Robards affair was both unsavory and messy. The captain had not been vacant in his threat to "invade II Nashville". He had arrived and left only the week before. He had consumed a substantial sampling from our local distillery, made a fool of himself several times in public, but avoided any contact with the Widow Donelson. It was apparent that he had received reliable information that Rachel had fled (*no one knew where*). It was also apparent that he had appreciated his good fortune -- that Andrew was not in residence either -- and had retreated hastily northward, back to Kentucky.

Insofar as I could determine, he did not have enough faith in the accuracy of his new cavalry pistols to test them out on an adversary as formidable as Andrew Jackson.

With a direct about-face, Robards headed straight for Virginia after permitting himself two days at his cabin in Kentucky to refresh his attire and tend to his chattels. Virginia, where he had several friends who were barristers, was the nearest state with statutes that related to separation and divorce. There, he had papers drawn up, notarized and formally presented in the courts as an "enabling act" opening the legal doors to divorce.

It was sometime in July, on a dead-hot afternoon, that Andrew Jackson received word through the court solicitor with whom he shared his office: Robards had filed legal papers in Virginia and the court had now given official approval. As might be expected -- and as Jackson could have recited it, letter and verse -- Robards had cited "adultery" as grounds for his action and had accused his "wayward wife of having lived in transport and in cohabitation with another man, an eligible bachelor for whom she had a romantic and immoral attachment."

Andrew Jackson raced out the door, leaped on his horse, and galloped like a demon possessed to the home of the Widow Donelson. Rachel had by this time returned safely from Natchez. She must hear the good news at once!

As befits the man of action that he was, Andrew immediately started making plans for his marriage to Rachel. I did not attend the wedding, a private affair held in the Donelson home. I wept two sets of tears that day: one in sorrow, admitting finally to myself that Andrew could never be mine; the other in joy, knowing that a heavy stone had been lifted from Rachel's heart at last and that she was free of the man she had come to detest and married to the man she loved.

That was in mid-August, 1791. One month later, I wept tears again, this time in an agony of disbelief. I had gone to visit my aunt to return a small locket. At first her maidservant would not let me in the door, protesting that her mistress was "in seclusion." When I insisted and quickly made my way to her chamber, sensing some family catastrophe, I found her tearful and distraught -- flung across the bed with her clothes in the greatest disarray.

"Whatever is the matter?" I asked in a breaking voice trembling over what her answer might be.

"It's…'tis Rachel and Andrew, ye must know. We have just been told they are not married after all. Captain Robards' divorce papers were never sealed by the court!"

Chapter 4

In the summer of 1791, as he made plans for his forthcoming marriage to Rachel Donelson Robards, Andrew Jackson purchased a modest plantation, Poplar Grove, on a hairpin turn of the Cumberland River, close to the town of Nashville. He had long wanted to become a landowner. Now, with unexpectedly substantial proceeds from his prospering law business and with a wedding in sight, he thought it a propitious time to make the initial investment.

Right after the marriage, I assisted my cousin Rachel in purchasing some dry goods and fashioning curtains for Poplar Grove. She was handy with needle and thread, having been properly schooled by my aunt. But she had a tendency to mismatch patterns and colors, with woeful results.

She would have found herself in a wretched situation, barely a few weeks into a new marriage. For Andrew, which *I* knew, but she did not -- had an intuitive discernment in matters relating to decoration and design. It surprised me that this was so, for a man brought up largely in wilderness settings. Yet it should not have, for I knew Andrew to be one who was constantly observing and questioning the relationships of things. Whether people or objects.

If he saw a set of Hepplewhite chairs in a dining room, he could not help wondering whether a French style might not look better.

If he rode by carpenters constructing a gambrel roof, he would pause briefly to reflect whether a Mansard style might not provide the owner with more space at little more effort.

If he met a handsome matron wearing a lavender gown at a ball, he instinctively closed his eyes for a few seconds, picturing her in wine-red.

That was Andrew.

Happily, Rachel was imaginative and alert. Once she found herself in her own home, she gave thought to matters of taste and art that had never occurred to her before.

"You are so helpful to me, Annie-Belle," she said to me one day when I had convinced her to discard one pair of bedroom curtains and stitch a replacement, using entirely different colors and fabrics.

"I want to please Andrew, since he is a caring man. Though I shrink from the idea of discarding brand new goods, I shall find another use for these pieces of handiwork; perhaps when we can afford to hire a maidservant."

With so much devotion infusing the marriage and the improvements to the home, it came as a stroke of lightning to learn that the marriage was invalid. Poplar Grove became a place that those antagonistic to Andrew (*and there were many such who had felt his legal arrows in court*) could point to in retaliation.

"Ya see that plantation smart by the river bend? Young couple lives there out of wedlock. And him a talker of law what shakes his finger at fellows not living quite by the book."

Rachel was for several weeks in a state of melancholy quite out of keeping with her nature. Her sisters and brothers were either confused or woebegone, depending upon their ages and degree of understanding. Her mother, my aunt, confined herself to her chambers for the better part of a month and was almost incoherent when friends tried to see and comfort her.

"My poor little dove," she kept repeating, "Her feathers have been plucked from her and she lies cold and naked in what was to have been her silk-lined nest. Oh, I cry for thee. And I pray that this hawk from Kentucky will not now swoop down on you again, talons out spread."

I was among those who attempted to reassure her about the future, though to little avail. She began to recover her senses only after the weeks began to pass and no "bird of prey" had flown in for an attack.

As for Andrew, he took the shattering news with remarkable equanimity. His first reaction was, of course, characteristically explosive. Fortunately, he received the dispatch, not at home, but at his office where it was delivered by a law clerk. In addition to the clerk, an innocent victim of the fulmination was a new client who had stopped by merely to sign a deed for a small parcel of land.

"For a moment," reported the client later, "I was shaken by the fear that Esquire Jackson had been disbarred or ordered to leave town. He all but popped the panes out of the window with his oaths."

"But then, do you know, he rapidly gained control of his emotions, cooled off his torrid language and was all apologies for having subjected me to such a fusillade.'"

Ahh, that was Andrew -- to the core. In truth, I think he looked on this unexpected reversal as a rollicksome new challenge, one to which he must now address every gram of his resourcefulness and ingenuity.

It was ironic (*that goes almost without saying*) that he, a lawyer, should have permitted himself to become so legally enmeshed. He was the first to admit this contrary state of affairs, perhaps even savoring the fact that he was -- as he liked to express it -- "no more than a common man, subject to the misjudgments and infirmities of any mortal."

When he learned that Robards had filed only for an enabling act, preliminary to filing for divorce, and had never pursued the matter further, he was suspicious.

Robards had probably precipitated the false report that Rachel was a free woman, knowing that Jackson would rush headlong into marriage, and consequently into an embarrassing social trap.

Notwithstanding the circumstances and misdoubts, Andrew survived it all in good temper, reasoning that he had attained his major objective: to consummate his love for Rachel. Everything else was of secondary importance. More than two years passed before divorce 'proceedings were finally instituted and the Robards-Donelson union dissolved.

Rachel and Andrew were remarried in 1794, by which time they had long been accepted by most people as husband and wife. Most people.

There was a drop of wormwood in the wine of harmony: Always there were those few people who did not accept -- and never *had* accepted -- the validity of the marriage. For them the second, and lawful, ceremony was meaningless. Rather than countervailing their contentions, the "real wedding" only seemed to goad Andrew's enemies into the most atrocious slanders.

Slander was a fever that was to flare up periodically throughout the Jackson's entire married life. It was, in fact, to contribute to the unholy tragedy that darkened Rachel's last illness and death.

Andrew Jackson could withstand almost every assault, verbal and physical, customarily expected by politicians, military officers, and other leaders in vulnerable positions. Yet he could not abide the slightest hint of in delicacy regarding his wife. If reference were made to her in a manner he considered slanderous or vengeful, he erupted in a volcanic rage and sometimes had to be forcefully restrained by his friends lest he endanger life and limb.

The intensity of the emotional tinderbox in which he lived was nowhere more graphically and dramatically illustrated than on that fateful day when we almost lost Andrew Jackson forever from this life and from the pages of American history.

Andrew's career had been impressive. By the end of the century he had, successively, been appointed to two judgeships, elected to the U.S. House of Representatives and then to the U.S. Senate, and acquired considerable wealth through speculations in land. In 1802, he was also appointed a major general in the militia of Tennessee, which had become a state six years earlier.

Thus it was that in 1806, he was a man of great national stature who, by his 39th year, had served his community, his state, and his country well.

Not everyone thought so. Among his most truculent detractors was Charles Dickinson, once referred to as "a 27 year-old dandy" and the best pistol shot in Tennessee. Life for him was empty unless he could goad an adversary into a duel or some other act of violence.

We almost lost you, Andrew Jackson -- all six feet of you and barely weighing 127 pounds after consuming a pint of heavy ale.

That was when Andrew's impetuosity nearly proved to be his undoing. He had been at odds with Dickinson for more years than I could remember. Heretofore, though, he had always been circumspect enough to tolerate the man's insolence. Up until the spring of 1806. That was when Dickinson had shown his disdain for the General by voicing deeply derogatory remarks about Rachel.

"How insatiable that tart must be," he is said to have declared in a barroom, "taking a second husband to bed while still married to the first one."

A verbal encounter with Dickinson was infuriating enough. But a physical encounter was more than likely to end in tragedy. His pistol had already killed six men in duels -- not counting several fatalities in less formal individual combat. He was as quick as a copperhead on the draw and so accurate in his aim that he could place four shots in succession so that they all targeted an area no greater than a silver dollar.

His favorite stunt before a duel, and right after arriving at the selected site, was legendary. He would hang a piece of string from a limb, then cut it with a single shot, leaving the evidence dangling to unnerve his adversary.

But Andrew -- bless him! -- was too preoccupied with his own sly artifices to pay attention to the wiles of "that reprobate, Charles." His first stratagem was to arrive late, winding and setting his bulbous gold watch after he had dismounted from his horse and hitched the animal to a tree. It gave the impression that he had been so little worried about the challenge and outcome that he had almost overlooked the engagement.

Andrew Jackson did not know it, nor did Dickinson or any of the two antagonists' seconds, but I, Annie Belle Donelson, was also on the scene. I had sneaked like a Seminole through a poplar copse and along a bramble thicket to a position where I could see quite clearly without readily being detected.

Why was I there? Andrew had not revealed to Rachel that he was about to fight a duel (*especially with Dickinson!*) So I knew that he would be alone on the field of battle, except for his second, John Overton. I was convinced that he would be killed. It was only fitting that he should have a woman "to hold his head and comfort him as he lay mortally wounded.

I plotted, too, what I might undertake at some future date to wreak revenge on Dickinson. He was an obnoxious and wretched creature who held ladies "in low esteem and said as much in the most scurrilous language.

Oh if I were only a man! I would practice with the pistols day and night for weeks on end, in fair weather and foul, until I had mastered every particular.

Then I would stride up to him in the most public place possible, slap him smartly across the cheek and announce, "Charles Dickinson, foe of womankind, I challenge you to an affair of honor!"

He would be astonished. He would rub his cheek. He would smirk with his insufferable self-confidence and smugness. He would accept. We would meet. And of course I would leave him bleeding mortally and in agony on the red-splattered grass.

What could a woman do? I would plot something, after we had buried Andrew with honor and love and life had become empty enough for me so that I would go to any lengths to avenge his murder.

When I peeped through the thicket and saw Andrew Jackson arrive and dismount, I was dumbfounded by his attire. I had already seen Mr. Dickinson appear on the scene promptly on the hour and shed his dark jacket.

After meticulously draping it over a low branch (where he expected to don it smartly after dispatching his opponent) he had stood waiting in a traditional dueling habit; a snug-fitting white lace shirt, tight knickerbockers, white hose and short boots.

But Mr. Jackson!

He arrived in a great coat that must have belonged to a gentleman three inches taller and seventy pounds heavier. With the lapels flaring up over his shoulders and his spindling, white stockinged legs descending below his black knickerbockers, he resembled an enormous vampire bat, ready to vault upwards into the air. The wheat-stalk hair, spiking upward from his arched brow, intensified the effect.

When he neither divested himself of the gray bulk of the garment nor seemed about to, one of Mr. Dickinson's two seconds raised a sharp voice of protest.

"Charles," he intoned, like a preacher damning the Devil, "You must demand that Jackson remove his cloak. It will distract your aim."

"Not at all," Dickinson assured him derisively, "I know right where I intend to place my bullet, camouflage or no. Besides, there is no protocol that forbids the wearing of an outer garment."

Hunching forward, so that he now seemed enfolded in fabric, Jackson busied himself with the case containing his brace of dueling pistols. He made quite a convincing drama, I can tell you, out of his apparent difficulty in opening the clasp. Had I not known him so well, I would surely have had the impression that it had been rusted tight for months, its owner not having been in a recent duel.

"What in the mark of Satan is the in an up to?" muttered Dickinson's other second, "Surely he must have his pistols more at the ready than he seems to make out!"

"With Jackson, you never can tell," commented the man who had voiced a protest, "You have to be wary of the scoundrel or he will confound you."

Dickinson himself, however, made no comment. I could see the annoyance, puckered with contempt that distorted his handsomely chiseled features ever so slightly.

When he finally drew forth the two pistols, Mr. Jackson was exasperatingly deliberate in his actions. He selected one and rubbed its barrel on the sleeve of his oversize greatcoat. He squeezed and released the grip several times, as though perhaps he were not truly familiar with it. All the while, he was thrusting his beetling jaw in the direction of the safety catch, then looking down his crooked nose at it, eyes narrowed.

Could it be that he had never noticed this appendage before!

'Are you ready, Mr. Jackson?" asked his second, John Overton, grown nervous and not looking forward to the bloodshed he was most certain to witness.

"In a minute, Sir, in a minute," replied Jackson in a voice deliberately squeaky and nasal, "my artillery is not so often brought into play as my opponent's, ya know." He squeezed his gaunt, shagbark cheeks with two fingers so that his lips were grotesquely pursed.

"Yes, yes, Mr. Jackson. I did not mean to discombobulate you at a moment like this."

What with all the motions and squintings and rubbings and squeezings, I could see that a bit of stage drama was being enacted directly across the greensward from my hiding place. I hoped that it was not lost on Mr. Dickinson who now stood with arms akimbo and one of his own ivory-handled pistols in hand.

I could see Andrew pluck a few pieces of lint from the arm of his coat, as though they distracted him. But all the time he was eyeing their fuzzy flight to note the drift (though slight) of the breeze. He cocked his angular head, too, in that characteristic manner, pretending to dislodge a speck of dust in one eye, yet using this feint to study the fronds atop a poplar to judge the force of the wind.

He seemed to be distracted by many things: the song of a Chickasaw wren in the brambles, the hollow pounding of hoofbeats on a clay trail a quarter of a mile distant, the fragrance of new-mown hay in the nearby pasture, which caused his nose to twitch.

Had I been close enough, I could have seen those blue eyes -- with the glint of hailstones now -- suddenly concentrate totally on his opponent; could have known that his sensitive ears had closed themselves to all save the click of Dickinson's pistol as he cocked it; could have watched his height increase an inch or two as he tautened himself to take the bullet that would most certainly penetrate skin and muscle.

"Are ye ready?" asked Overton a second time, noting that the two adversaries were precisely in position eight paces -- or 24 feet -- from each other.

I am, Sir," barked Dickinson cooly.

"I am ready," echoed Jackson, in his scratchiest voice.

"Fere!" roared Overton in his old country dialect.

Almost before the man had bitten off the command, Dickinson had raised his pistol and fired.

"Oh, my God I" I moaned, so loudly that my cry must surely have been heard. I had seen a puff of dust instantly come and go in that part of the cloak's fabric hiding Andrew's left chest where his heart must be.

"The Devil!" bellowed Dickinson, "Have I missed the man?" He was so undone for a brief moment that he teetered slightly off the mark where his feet had been planted.

Andrew Jackson remained as stiff and still as an icicle. Then he pressed his left arm tightly against his chest. He had felt the ball tear into his flesh. Whether the wound were mortal or no, he was still erect, and conscious. Slowly and deliberately, as though numbed, he raised his right arm and brought his pistol to bear on Dickinson.

Had he planned it this way, knowing that it would have been impossible to outdraw the younger man? His long, thin fingers seemed to wrap themselves around the grip, like the legs of an enormous spider.

Painfully, he squeezed the trigger. The hammer sprang forward but stopped at half cock.

"Damnation!" exclaimed Jackson, "Damnation!"

All the while Dickinson stood there defiantly, compelled by the dueler's code of honor to remain in position until the single shot had been fired. When the hammer clicked, he flinched, almost unnoticeably. Jackson drew the hammer back, aimed again, and squeezed the trigger. This time the powder fired and Dickinson took the shot below the ribs in the vicinity of the groin. He dropped to the grass, bleeding profusely.

Though his seconds rushed to his aid to stem the flow of blood, Dickinson's hours were numbered. He was dead by nightfall.

From my hiding place (still undiscovered) I witnessed a remarkable test of courage and will. Andrew appeared to be unharmed. Still in his great gray cloak, he returned the pistols to their case, took the grip in hand and strode to his horse, accompanied by Overton but leaving the others to attend to the fallen man.

"It is a miracle!" I gasped, "He is untouched. The cloak must have made it impossible for the sharp-eyed Dickinson to sight on a vulnerable portion of his body.

Little did I know then that Andrew, whom I had never expected to see leave the dueling grounds alive, had taken the bullet barely an inch from his heart. The lead ripped the chest muscles, broke two ribs, and came to rest in the left lung. He was forced to convalesce for the better part of five weeks and for the rest of his life paid agonizingly for this victory. He was given to coughing up pus and blood on frequent occasions. Surgeons who examined his skinny chest years later with the intention of removing the bullet and clearing up this had to admit defeat.

"Did you know how gravely you were wounded?" I asked Andrew some weeks later when he was finally getting back on his feet.

"I judged it worse than it actually was," he admitted, "but I'd sell me nose to the Devil before I'd have given Charles Dickinson the satisfaction of knowing he had wounded me."

"Even though he was dying?"

"Dying? My dear Annie-Belle, it was a state that was long overdue for him. He had insulted Rachel in a foul manner -- blasphemed a lady who could neither understand his malevolence nor retaliate.

"Had he shot me directly through the heart, I should yet have retained enough of the spark of life to go through with my plan: to take the most careful, deliberate aim and make sure that my target was not missed."

I have never been one to believe in superhuman feats, ones that defy God's design for mortal man. Yet I am convinced that Andrew was one man who could have miraculously staved off Death itself long enough to effect his purpose.

Odious though Charles Dickinson was, his enmity was nothing compared with the subtle and long-standing malevolence of Andrew's greatest Nemesis, Henry Clay.

Chapter 5

All Soul's Eve, the night of October 31, 1809. was a time to remember with awe.

A galloping storm had ridden from the Appalachians southwestward into Tennessee, across the Great Smokies, whipping the winding waters of the Cumberland near Nashville into a watery rope. Thunder roared and lightning flashed. The lightning seemed to rebound from peak to peak and crag to crag in the hills surrounding the town rather than striking in its normal fashion.

Two like events occurred that night: the births of babies, one male, one female. They took place in areas as topographically and socially different as could be imagined.

The girl was born west of town in a wilderness outpost commonly known as White Oak Flat because of its stand of ragged oaks on a plateau. The birth took place in obscurity for the mother was unmarried, one-fourth Chickasaw, and the father an itinerant trapper from Kentucky who was never seen again after the night of conception. The baby came from the warmth of the womb into a world of terrifying conditions. Several oaks were sent crashing by the violence of the wind, one barely missing the small cabin in which the mother huddled.

"Becky Hayes. 'Tis your name, little one," whispered the mother after the tempest had romped westward and her fright had dissolved.

She was not Rebecca or Becky-Anne. Just Becky. She had enough Indian blood in her to be endowed with ebony eyes and hair as dark as a raven. Yet she had a fair, rosy complexion, said to come from Welsh stock in the family.

The other birth occurred in one of the finest homes in Nashville, on the banks of the Cumberland, amidst elegant surroundings and properly announced with toasts of claret and nips of brandy. The storm, though muffled by the delicate trills of harpsichord and flute in the dining salon, was enough noted so that the father of Truxton Blair, newborn, later prophesied over cordials and cigars that the storm was auspicious.

"My son," he said proudly, holding up a robust infant with blue eyes and wisps of blonde hair "will be a doughty general, his sword already tempered by the forge of lightning across the Big Ridge.

The mother, retired to the drawing room with several matrons, prophesied that the thunder imbued her infant with the tongue of an orator.

The midwife, her responsibilities fulfilled, retired to her bed chamber and yanked the draperies as tightly as she could across the casements. Lucifer fire was sparking in the cold night air outside. It was All Soul's Eve and nothing wholesome could be augured for an infant born in the bowels of God's fury. Besides, the lightning was so close she could smell the very brimstone in the atmosphere. She had heard said that slivers of lightning could penetrate cracks and pervade a room with its smothering odor of sulfur.

Some days later, Andrew and Rachel Jackson heard about the birth of Truxton Blair, for the parents were well known to them. As for Becky (later *renamed Rebecca but always called Becky*) her circumstances and fortunes remained as obscure and secretive as her birth. It would be many years before her name would be as familiar to Andrew as that of young Truxton.

It was one of those ironies of life -- even more so perhaps than the bizarre misjudgments surrounding the divorce proceedings that Andrew and Rachel were unable to beget children of their own. They were so almightily interested in young people, and so desirous of being surrounded by the bright faces of youth.

"You should have married young Jackson," said my mother to me one day, "You would have filled his home with babies!"

Well, I knew that. And I had used my wiles without so much as jiggling the scales of love. I was happy, though, when Andrew legally adopted his nephew, Andy, whose parents were in such financial straits that they could no longer support or educate him. Although I referred to Rachel as one of the "Young in Heart" at the time she was being courted, it was really Andy who personified what was to become a vein in the Jackson heritage.

Although I was 33 at the time Becky Hayes and Truxton Blair were born and 34 when Andy was taken into the household, I suppose you could say that "Annie-Belle reflected the *spirit* of the Young in Heart."

Yet that could have been said about Andrew, many times over.

What I am really leading up to is an opportunity to voice my abhorrence for Henry Clay, the man whom I considered Andrew Jackson's greatest though not always most recognized adversary.

Clay was a personality who radiated charm, a genial Kentuckian, and one of the nation's most articulate orators -- he was to be called by some our country's greatest statesmen -- though he never did achieve his real ambition: the Presidency. He was as polished as a mahogany banister on a Federal stairwell by comparison with the split-rail brashness of Mr. Jackson.

Nonetheless, he was always suspect in my opinion for one powerful reason: He neither liked nor understood young people. Since that attitude was as far from Jackson's as the Allegheny was from the Loosahatchie, there were bound to be hard feelings. I think the man really began to rankle about the time the Jacksons moved into the Hermitage and for the first time there was a refuge for young people of all ages who were either orphaned or cast adrift by incompetent elders.

It festered in Clay's mind, too, that a man of national prominence could be deeply emotional, sometimes sentimental, and almost as ingrained a romanticist at heart as the late-lamented poet, Robert Burns.

"Hell and brimstone!" exclaimed Clay one day, on hearing that Andrew and Rachel had adopted a homeless Indian child. "That man has sugarplums in his head instead of brains, and syrup in his veins in place of blood!"

The trouble with Clay was that I do not think he ever had been a boy. He simply popped from infancy to adulthood and began making speeches. Andrew, on the other hand, never stopped being a boy for the rest of his life. He continued to remember with a chuckle many of the practical jokes he had perpetrated back during his days in North Carolina. Characteristic was the time when he was attending dancing school. The schoolmistress, for some reason known only to God, appointed him chairman of the annual Christmas Ball. He secretly sent invitations to the Wood sisters, widely recognized as "the town's fanciest prostitutes."

When they arrived, as radiantly garbed as peacocks, the orchestra wheezed to a halt, the boys and girls giggled, and two of the chaperoning matrons promptly fainted.

It was another one of the intriguing Jackson contradictions that he, a lover of babies and children who could spend hours with them enjoying the most juvenile games, could also be a brilliant Major General in the Regular Army, an Indian fighter of note, and the hero of the Battle of New Orleans, during which he thoroughly whipped the British.

"The Hermitage is almost finished."

It was in the spring of 1819 that I heard this welcome report. Andrew and Rachel had purchased 650 acres of land some twelve miles northeast of Nashville. At the time, the rolling terrain contained one small, block-shaped house with three rooms and several outbuildings of little consequence. Over the years, Andrew planned and built a mansion, inspired by the design of George Washington's home, Mount Vernon. The building was two stories high, with six fluted wooden columns rising from the base to the thick, flat roof. The original structure was converted to servants' quarters.

His pleasure at the refinements of design and tastefulness of the furnishings was exceeded only by his delight with the concept of space. Inside, there was room for many guests, permanent and transient. Outside, there were endless fields and pastures and woodlands, ponds and streams, riding trails and gardens.

"The place is anemic right now," Andrew apologized to me one day that summer when my aunt and I paid our first visit to the Hermitage, "But we'll have some blood coursing through it anon. Andrew, Jr., will be back from school come the end of the month. My little Indian, Lincoyer, will also be in residence. I sent him East to Richmond with my groom, to purchase a pair of Shetlands for the children's stable."

Lincoyer was a Creek who had been orphaned by one of the General's own actions. He was about to be killed by the women of the tribe, according to Indian custom, to join his parents in the Great Beyond. But Andrew had scooped him up in front of his saddle and trotted the terrified child to his command tent. Later, he learned English and was legally made a ward of the Jacksons.

"Yes," mused Andrew, "you will see some youthful frolicking around this fine home. I also intend to adopt Truxton and bring him here."

"Truxton? But surely his mother and father are wealthy enough to ..."

"Ah, you had not heard Annie-Belle. Colonel and Mrs. Blair were lost at sea when the Royal Glen struck a reef off Nantucket and sank while sailing for Boston."

Andrew did begin to invite young people to visit the Hermitage, as he had planned. Truxton, unfortunately, was not among them, since he was assigned by the courts to the care of an aging Aunt in Nashville. By this time, he was a lad of ten, his eyes as blue as they had been at birth, his hair golden and ringed with tight curls that were the envy of young maidens whose locks were obstinately straight.

"I would keep an eye on the boy," I suggested some months later, on learning about the situation, "for he will soon be too manly to remain in the care of a crotchety old lady whose health, I understand, is slipping steadily."

"That I shall, that I shall," he agreed.

"If I may take the liberty, Sir," I added, "I have another suggestions to make...

"By all means." He grasped my upper arm lightly with his long, spindly fingers and looked at me expectantly."

"There is also a young lady well, she is a child, too, the same age as Truxton who might merit your attention. Oh, I do not see this as anything immediate, Mr. Jackson, but a measure you might wish to consider three or four years hence. The girl's name is Becky Hayes, born out of wedlock to an impoverished woman who has a cabin and a patch of land some miles to the west of here.

"There is some Indian blood here. The child is a free spirit who can ride bareback across the fields and along the trails like a young chief. I understand, too, that she can outrun and out-wrestle boys her age and a little older.

"Why wait, Annie-Belle?" asked Andrew, quickly intrigued by my description. "The lass would be like a breeze in the forest here. She could have her own pony and challenge Lincoyer to races."

"I wish the child were ready for such a change. But it is too soon. She is an only child and her mother desperately needs her. The poor woman is lonely and I'm afraid has been taking to the bottle. She is a proud person though, and has rejected several offers of assistance. She would sooner die than give up Becky for adoption."

"We shall play a waiting game, then. I count on you to monitor the situation for me and advise me when circumstances so warrant."

Andrew Jackson busied himself with improvements at the Hermitage over the next few years that is, when he could spare the time from a multitude of duties on behalf of the State and the Republic. He was for a brief, and unhappy period appointed Governor of the Florida Territory, resigning mainly because Rachel could not tolerate the enervation of the climate and constantly longed for the more temperate breath of the Cumberlands.

He was also elected again to the United States Senate, a responsibility he would have discharged with never-ending relish had it not dislodged him so frequently from the Hermitage, and away from the companionship of a wife who could not endure the Potomac.

Lastly, he permitted the Tennessee legislature to persuade him to inaugurate a campaign for the Presidency.

It was, and I knew this even more acutely than Andrew himself, the ultimate sacrifice. His acquiescence was also one of those provocative Jacksonian contradictions. Everything he held dear home, wife, friends, woodlands and mountains was in Tennessee. Everything he detested--bureaucracy, social sham, shallow political foes, debilitating climate was in Washington.

"Why, Sir," I asked him bluntly a few weeks after the legislature had publicly proclaimed its persuasiveness, "did you ever agree to throw yourself into a race that offers nothing but heartaches and headaches as its reward?"

"Well you should ask," he sighed, "The venture is like mounting a two-headed horse and not knowing in which direction you will be propelled. You might say the prognosis is that A. Jackson is losing his mind. Yet it has always been my folly, to aspire to the Presidency. Did you not suspect that all along?"

I could not deny it. One had only to know what kinds of sparks kindled the man to understand his determination to move from the plough to the Presidency. Yet he had one tragic blind spot: He could not foresee how devastating his decision would eventually be for Rachel.

Rachel was partially blind, too. As the campaign heated up during the early months of 1828, she basked if modestly in its glow. I still have the note I received from her one day, regretting that she could not attend a little supper we were giving for Truxton Blair who, though yet only 18, was being indoctrinated into the law by a group of local barristers.

"Oh, my dear friend, how shall I ever get through this bustle? From 40 to 50 personages call at the Hermitage each day on one business or other. It tires my blood. Some are much to be enjoyed. Like Mr. Lafayette. He wears a wig and is inclined to corpulence. Very healthy. Eats hearty. Goes to every party. Most are tiresome, yet we have to conduct pleasantries with all."

So innocent and trusting she was, amidst the "bustle."

It startled me to see how nasty the campaign was turning as it moved into the fall. Henry Clay was behind the most vicious attacks on Andrew Jackson, though he usually hid behind that bastardly smile of his and let his underlings shovel the filth.

"Ought a convicted adultress and her paramour husband be placed in the highest offices of this free and Christian land?"

The slur, published by an editor who was a tool of Clay's, was typical. Andrew was furious, and even more so because no holds were barred during political campaigns and candidates could be vilified wantonly without fear of inciting a duel. He reacted with Cyclopean outbursts of denunciation, which whipped his constituents into a frenzy of cheering.

But poor Rachel!

She was undone. On one occasion, while she was in a neighbor's home helping to serve tea at a political rally, she overheard two ladies gossiping about her as an "illiterate country woman." When I came upon her, she was crouching in a corner, hysterical and terrified.

"Come now, Cousin Rachel," I scolded her in a manner intended to make light of the matter, "you can see they are bumpkins, jealous of your eminence."

I promptly escorted her home. Halfway to the Hermitage, she insisted on dismounting at a stream, to flush the tears from her eyes so that Andrew might not suspect her grief.

Right then, I had a premonition that Rachel Jackson would never see the inside of the White House.

Chapter 6

When it became evident that Andrew Jackson had been elected President during the balloting in November, 1828, the quiet city of Nashville was transformed into a sprawling encampment.

Andrew's plan was to depart from the Hermitage on December 23, the anniversary of the Night Battle, Consequently, old soldiers, Indian scouts, military officers, and retired veterans flowed into town in every conceivable conveyance or afoot. Legislators, contingents of the militia, professional societies, commercial federations, and other such bodies all vied with each other in the planning of a "Continuous Ovation" that would take place from Nashville all along the 820 miles to Washington.

A North Carolinian volunteered to drive the General and his Lady the distance in a golden coach with six white horses. Overwhelmed, frightened, and confused, Rachel wanted no coach, no white horses, no echoing throngs. Retreating into a kind of pious cocoon she had threaded about her during the recent, unsettling months, she somehow began equating the forthcoming leap into Greatness as sinful.

I had rather be a doorkeeper in the House of God," she told me one day, "than live in that palace in Washington."

Her hands felt hot to the touch. Her brow was feverish. I called softly for her maidservant. We induced her to go to her chamber to rest, and even to swallow one of Andrew's favorite elixirs that was said to reduce humors when troops were stricken in the swamps.

Within a day or two, she was back on her feet, her face and extremities normal to the touch.

That was in early December. On December 17, I was at the edge of Nashville Square, just climbing into my gig to return home with some purchases, when a horseman galloped down the cobbled street and reined up to me in a froth.

"Where is the office of Dr. Samuel Hogg?" he asked, panting heavily.

"You are right on it," I replied in alarm, "Whatever is the matter?"

"It's Mrs. Jackson. She is in spasms."

He hastened towards the doorway where I had pointed, while I half leaped, half tumbled out of the gig to follow. Fortunately, Dr. Hogg was in residence, as was his assistant, young Dr. Heiskell. We made a sight startling to pedestrians as they, astride three horses, and I in the gig sped northeastward out of town.

We found Rachel lying on her bed, her face contorted with pain and her chest and left shoulder heaving spasmodically. Andrew had called in a country physician, who had bled the patient once without easing her distress. The doctor, quite elderly and little accustomed to such elegant surroundings, had not located the proper vein. When Dr. Hogg repeated the operation with professional composure, my cousin noticeably began to relax and show signs of great relief.

Exhausted, she soon fell asleep in her high French bed. "I shall sit with Mrs. Jackson," said Andrew quite sternly I thought refusing my offer to spell him.

By morning, Rachel was cheerful, manifestly on the mend and with her pain greatly diminished. I was permitted in the sickroom for barely three minutes, but long enough to scold myself for having envisioned the dear lady on her way to the grave.

Three days later, on Sunday evening, December 22, Rachel was confined again to her bed, this time with a rheum and catarrh. Andrew was advised by the physician to sleep in an adjoining room lest he too be infected. Twice she awoke and was assisted by the maid to the fireplace to overcome chills that were racking her body. At about dawn she collapsed and the servant's screams raised Andrew and the rest of the household.

Andrew held his wife fondly in his arms. But she was gone.

"Bleed her, bleed her!" he pleaded with Dr. Hogg. The operation was performed by this good man as deftly as on the previous occasion. Barely two drops flowed to discolor the gauze pressed against the incision. Her face was as white as the sheet on which she lay. Her beautiful dark eyes were open, staring at the ceiling as though she were a Greek statue. Dr. Hogg gently closed them with his fingers and bowed his head.

She was buried in the garden, 150 paces from the East door of the Hermitage.

It was said that 10,000 people attended Rachel's funeral -- a third of them on foot and the rest in buggies, carriages, coaches, farm wagons, every manner of rig, every breed of saddle horse, work horse, and pony.

I am haunted by the strange realization that I do not remember any people at all at the funeral. The only image I have in mind is that of Andrew Jackson, standing tall and bareheaded above the casket. Yes, there was movement all about him and stretching as far as the eye could see, and beyond. But the movement was like that of a heaving, many-colored sea on which the sun was glinting, distorting the human vision and changing the real world into an unearthly setting.

He seemed to be taller than ever before, as though he were being stretched upward by some celestial power. His straight hair, now turned white as frost, rose like a bishop's miter above his rimpled brow.

Sam Houston led the pallbearers.

The Reverend William Hume spoke for 20 minutes.

Plans for the overland parade to Washington had, of course, long since been dashed. Instead, Andrew announced that he would travel to the nation's capital alone, quietly, and by boat. In mid-January, 1829, he was driven by carriage in the coldest of weather to Fort Adams (which had just been Mississippi renamed Memphis). On the 18th, he stepped aboard a river boat, the same on which he regularly loaded cotton from the Hermitage plantation for shipment to the East Coast.

My heart ached for you, Andrew, in your loneliness.

My passionate, compulsive, romantic love for you of times past had long since been mellowed into the fine wine of endearment. Yet that mutation did not assuage my pain. Passionate love can be a fierce and often frightening emotion. Yet compassion can sear the heart in its own unrelenting way. Though some of your enemies rejoiced to see your spirit quenched and you in misery, there were those of us who rightly envisioned your particular kind of Hell.

It was not just the void -- many a man has lost a mate, unexpectedly and tragically, and carried on. It was the fact that, at the very time that your world had been yanked out from under your feet, your shoulders were expected to bear the most awesome responsibilities in the Land.

As the awkward paddles began to churn and the steamboat headed down river, dark clouds swirled menacingly over the Mississippi. Those who looked to nature for auguries, shook their heads solemnly and remarked that the departure boded nothing but ill for the administration of the President-to-be. Others, interpreting things more realistic than oracular, opined that Andrew Jackson would never survive his first term of office.

Their reasoning was sound. Andrew, at 61, was not only despondent and in a poor mental state, but suffered from a distressing barrage of physical ailments. These included chronic dysentery, bone infections, lung abscesses, colitis, arthritis, and the vestiges of tuberculosis not to mention a variety of scars from wounds and injuries, two bullets still lodged in his body, failing sight in one eye, dental problems that limited his diet, and incessant migraine headaches. He was also plagued by severe insomnia.

I must have been alone in the conviction that Andrew would not only survive, but would bring to the Presidency dimensions not yet known to that high office. Few people even suspected, let alone understood, the intensity of his will power, his lifelong belief that he could not fail in any endeavor to which he set his mind.

Dark-browed and despondent though he looked on the day he paid a visit to Rachel's grave and departed from the Hermitage, I could picture a shining light far ahead of him. My optimism stemmed from a seemingly bread-and-butter conversation we exchanged the week before his leave-taking.

"Tell me, Annie-Belle," he said, catching me somewhat by surprise when I was helping my cousins with packing and storing some of Rachel's effects, "what do you hear about young Truxton Blair these days?"

"He is proceeding well with his internship in law, Sir, and will be ready to go into practice on his own soon."

"Good, good. He is now 20 years old?"

"Less a few months, Mr. Jackson."

"Handsome, I'll wager. Like his late father."

"Comely, in an unconventional way. His nose and lips are irregular, so that if you view him from two different angles you get two slightly different images. His hair is blonde like his mother's and as curly as the fronds of a budding fern."

"A pity, a pity" said Andrew with a sad shake of his head and rubbing his own singular growth, "I know how that can be endless teasing from one's peers."

"The curls became him as a young child, but were an annoyance after he reached his tenth birthday. His French tutor called him <u>Contourné</u>, 'Curly-Wurly,' a term that sent him into spasms of anger if repeated by other school boys.

"However, I should add that by the time he was 16 or so he discovered that his curlicues held great attraction for the opposite sex. If you will forgive an intimacy, I understand that last year he was the paramour of a lady several years his senior who delighted in running her fingers through his curls, pulling them straight, and moistening them with kisses."

"Ah-ha! That is the secret of success: to turn a sow's ear into silk." His lips flickered with the first smile I had seen on his face since Rachel's illness. But it vanished on the instant and he gave me a bristling, serious look.

"The foot. Tell me about that."

I knew immediately what he referred to. Truxton had been born with a lame left foot, a deformity not visible to the layman's eye. It had been detected only after the infant, at the age of some 14 months, was ungainly and halting in his first attempts to walk. (Was it the result of brimstone in the air the night of his birth? Perhaps the midwife had been foresighted in her fears.

"He has overcome the handicap to a remarkable extent." I explained, "He started taking long hikes largely over the roughest terrain he could find -- from the time he was seven or eight years old. He will always have a limp and be slower than others in feats of running. Yet he is far above average in the strength of his lower limbs and his endurance."

"I am relieved to hear that, Annie-Belle. For I want to get the lad to Washington. And the last thing any one wants in that city is a knot in the reins when starting out."

"Washington, Sir? But he seems to be poised for an admirable career in Nashville."

"The plan, Annie-Belle, the plan! Have you forgotten our conversations in the past about my desire to give young people a *better* home, more opportunities for growth and development in all things?"

"But, Sir, we were talking about the Hermitage about Andrew, Jr., your nephew, and Lincoyer, and those others of the eleven you and Mrs. Jackson took under your roof..."

"Aye. We were." He thrust his jaw directly at me and I could see a new sparkle in those eyes that had gazed recently on so much anguish.

"And what is wrong with the White House "

The White House! It had never occurred to me not until that instant that he pictured the Young in Heart among the familial occupants of the President's mansion. Not only pictured, but pressed the issue. Was the aunt still alive? Was the young man living at her home? Had he ever been to the capital of the Republic?

No, the aunt died during the summer, after a lingering struggle with dropsy... No, Truxton had moved into a rooming house in the city... Possibly he had been to Washington, but he has made no mention of seeing his future there."

I could barely keep up with his questions.

"A shame I did not know about these circumstances. I should have liked to have seen him at the Hermitage."

I apologized for not having brought the subject to his attention, excusing myself on the grounds that the heat of the Presidential campaign had been too withering to permit attention to any other issues.

He dashed right past my comment.

"I place this matter in your hands, Annie-Belle, to approach this young man at the proper time and with your canny gift of persuasion. I shall not rest until you tell me that he has agreed to take up residence in the White House."

Before I could acquiesce or demur, he had plunged into the next subject.

"Becky Hayes where do we stand on her?"

"I have been out of touch. You must forgive me, Mr. Jackson, but she lives almost 20 miles west of here. And we have almost no lines of communication."

When he persisted, I told him what little I knew about Becky: Her mother had died a year or so ago. The circumstances were clouded. There had been problems with hard drink, liver and stomach complaints, aggravated by near-starvation much of the time. After burying her mother, Becky had bartered the cabin and land for a carriage and some clothing and had gone northwest a few miles to Fort Clark. There, she was serving as maidservant to the wife of a major.

"I know only that she detested the job and had hoped to save enough money to move to Nashville or farther east.

The major was an Indian fighter and constantly ridiculing the 'dung-smeared savages' and the 'slatternly squaws' to her face, leering and sometimes pawing her. You can imagine how she would feel, one-eighth Indian herself and more proud of that side of her family than the Welsh."

"Damnation! Damnation!" Andrew exploded, pounding his right fist against the palm of his left hand so hard I thought he must have snapped a bone. "We must pluck that flower from the bed of thorns, and as soon as possible.

"I suppose," he added gloomily, "that the poor child is stooped and scarred beyond restitution."

"Not at all, Sir, On that point I am happy to report that she is one of those glorious beings able to thrive on adversity. When I saw her last, barely three months ago, she was just turned 19, blushingly healthy, with jet black hair that reached to her waist and the deepest, richest, brownest eyes you could imagine. Her skin was nut brown, as soft as satin, her features delicate. Yet I understand she can spend all day in the saddle on the scraggiest trails and dismount at sundown looking as fresh as though she had stepped from her boudoir."

"Dammit, Young Lady (*He called me that until I was in my mid-60s*), Becky Hayes has the pedigree we want around the White House! How much do you want to find her, fetch her, and bundle her off to Washington?" He thrust a lanky forearm deep into the recesses of his cloak and yanked forth the gold-tooled leather <u>portemonnaie</u> that the Marquis de Lafayette had presented to him on the occasion of his political victory.

"Will two hundred dollars be enough?"

I could hardly stifle the outburst of laughter that welled within me. It was the contradictory Andrew to the core. He had suffered the greatest loss in his life; he was in a state of overwhelming depression; he faced the most backbreaking challenges any individual could be called upon to surmount; he was sure to be surrounded by more enemies than friends once he relieved John Quincy Adams of the burdens of the Presidency.

Yet his overriding concern was how to persuade the Young in Heart to go to Washington and enliven the staid facade of the Executive Mansion.

Yes, I could see a real glow of light at the end of that long, dark tunnel.

Chapter 7

Andrew Jackson stood alone at his inauguration. Bareheaded.

His stiff white hair brandishing his loneliness. "I do, so help me God.

"I will, with the blessing of the Almighty..." His replies, as the oath of office was administered were in the singular. Yet his mind was in the plural. For in every instance he pictured Rachel standing there beside him. In his mind, his response was not "I," but "We."

Once again, as at the funeral, he seemed to be there in isolation and solitude -- despite the undulating waves of people, flowing across the Washington landscape as far as the eye could see.

I was not at the inauguration that chilly March afternoon in 1829. Most of us his distant cousins and nephews and nieces had remained in Nashville, because of the unsettled conditions in the nation's capital. Some three weeks later, however, I received correspondence from

Andrew through the courtesy of a young naval officer returning home on leave.

You cannot imagine, friend Annie-Belle, how ludicrous it all was. Some thousands of souls had repaired to the White House and grounds after the Inauguration -- most of 'them visitors from afar expecting to view a huge Spectacle. Some few being told it was proper upon the installation of a new President to wish him well.

While I appreciated the sentiment, I cannot say that I relished the adventure. The mob scene was made up of All Creation, the edifice, the porticos, the turf being jammed with celebrants.

Inside, where I was supposed to greet and say a few words to my fellow citizens, all was pandemonium. One country fellow of weight about 200 pound sat astride a harpsichord (I believe it a purchase of Pres. & Mrs. Adams) butting the keys as though they were drum heads.

The ornate fireplace in the East Room was a bucolic setting a woody fellow in buckskin roasting a hare on a wooden stake.

The toasts were many, though more wine seemed to end up on the carpet than in the gullet.

Andrew's descriptions continued in this vein for two full pages, written in that skiltering hand of his, with his mind always a sentence ahead of his quill.

On one occasion, he was approached by a stranger who, having no idea whatsoever as to Jackson's identity, asked "where the dueling grounds might be found?" When Andrew seemed perplexed, the stranger persisted.

"This Jackson, you know, is lightning on the trigger.

He intends to challenge to a duel any Senator rash enough to oppose his political acts!"

In another instance, he was approached by a hulking laborer who looked at his pasty face and sickly figure somewhat doubtfully.

"General Jackson, I guess?"

"Yes, Sir, I am none other."

"Why they told me you was dead."

"No, not yet. Providence has hitherto preserved my life."

"And is your wife alive, too?"

"No," replied Andrew, shaking his head mournfully. "Aye," replied the workman with a gleam of understanding lighting his eyes, "I thought it was one or t'other of ye."

The ovation for the new President was like nothing ever seen before in the nation's capital or elsewhere.

Since Andrew had no close relatives, no wife, no children, the People had decided to adopt him as father, brother, son. The poor man I Though overcome with emotion at the affection shown him by these adoring masses, the intensity of it all was too much for him. As he wrote:

To escape the Saturnalia, I slipped through a back hallway and up to the room I believed had been designated the Presidential bed chamber. To my dismay, it had been taken over by a boisterous group of Potomac rivermen who thought I was from the wine cellar, come to take orders.

Hastily, I backed out, retiring to a closet-sized file room I had noticed nearby. It was vacant save for an elderly bookkeeper who seemed half blind as he pinched out figures on a ledger. Is there an inn close at hand, I queried him, where a traveler might find a night's lodging.

"No...", he grunted. Then added that I might try the "Wigwam" down the road, since the innkeeper's rates were too exorbitant for the likes of most visitors in town. By good fortune, he thought to explain that the name was really Gadsby's Tavern.

Grabbing a small portmanteau, I hastily repaired to Gadsby's. The availability of a room was explained by the usurious rate. The clerk took my name, wrote "Jackson, A." on a scrap of paper and handed it to a small boy who showed me to my cubicle.

The bed linens were not what I might have enjoyed at the White House. But exhaustion makes a good pillow and I was asleep in no time.

After the inauguration, the better part of a month passed before the White House was restored to its former state.

It was during this period, in late March, when one of my several cousins, Andrew Jackson Donelson, was informed that a young man had arrived at the East door of the White House and was seeking entrance. Donelson had been appointed Presidential secretary, while his wife served as the official White House hostess.

"I am Truxton Blair," said the visitor when ushered into the smallish office on the ground floor, "from Tennessee."

"Blair? Oh yes, I remember the Colonel, your late father. What is your business?"

"Did not the President mention me ? I am taking up residence here. In the White House, that is.

"Of course, I do remember now. There are so many businesses to attend to these days." He swept his hand in an arc, indicating mounds of papers and missives. "Why don't you just go in? The President likes informality."

He walked to the rear of the office and opened a narrow door. "Straight down there and to the left."

Truxton felt his tongue go limp as he groped along a dank, unlit corridor and tried to frame the words he would say to the great man. He expected to come upon a large, sumptuous office. Perhaps an aide would meet him and he would have to sit in an ante room for some minutes before being ushered in. Not so. He abruptly found himself in a modest study with a lone occupant.

The desk was disappointingly small, its dark walnut gouged and scarred as though perhaps it had seen service in field tents during military service. The top was a confusion of documents, tattered books, glass vials, a pewter pitcher, and several miniature portraits. The man behind this hotch-potch wore a dark, somewhat dusty suit with oval-shaped lapels, high collar, and a gray ruffled shirt with a very full neck-scarf. The white hair sprouting from his wrinkled pate identified him immediately as Mr. Jackson.

He looked more scholarly than military, almost like a preacher preparing his Sunday sermon. Indeed, he clutched a ragged Bible in both hands, cupped up almost to chin level so that he could read it through a pair of glasses so tiny they seemed more like those of a child.

What did journalists see in this man that prompted them to equate him with "flashes of lightning" and "actions like thunderbolts?"

Andrew Jackson looked up, ever so slowly, pushing the glasses down to the tip of his craggy nose with his right hand. The eyes were moist as though something in the scriptures had stirred his emotions.

"Excuse me, Sir... Mr. President."

"I await your pleasure. Who are ye?"

"Truxton Blair, Sir. The son of the late Colonel Blair who, with my mother, was lost at sea."

"Yes, yes. You were but a child when I saw you last. Come closer. My sight is not what it used to be and I see everything foreshortened like a field mouse trying to sight a sparrow at the top of a tree.

Truxton laughed inwardly at thought of this old warrior playing the part of a field mouse. He suddenly felt quite comfortable in the presence of greatness, and almost eager to engage in conversation.

The two men talked, sometimes animatedly, for the better part of half an hour. Andrew was delighted to learn that his new ward had already arranged for employment with a small law firm on New York Avenue, only a few blocks from the executive mansion.

"What is most opportune," explained Truxton, "is that the partners are mainly engaged in interpreting Congressional legislation for their clients. Thus, I shall be thrust into that area that most captures my fancy: the world of politics.

"Politics! Well you are in the right pond for that. Just don't swim too close to the alligators!"

Truxton Blair, more than any of the other wards (and wards-to-be) of Andrew Jackson, had a certain feistiness of nature that lured him towards the "alligator lairs." I think that was what attracted Andrew most to the young man, for he saw in him something of his own contrary nature and love of a good fight. It was evident that Truxton was politically naive, certainly a greenhorn when it came to dealing with Washington legislators. Yet this encouraged Andrew all the more.

"You are starting with a clean slate and an open mind, young man," he advised, "so be your own man. Be all ways aggressive in pursuit of what you feel is best for your state and your country.

"Every great man is marked by hearty self-reliance; every failure is caused by self-mistrust. So be inner-directed, Truxton Blair. Set your own standards of conduct from within. Explore the high sierras of the mind, yet do not let yourself be clouded from reality."

His voice deepened and he looked upward, as though seeing far beyond the confines of the room. Then he caught himself abruptly, blinked, and looked straight at his visitor.

"Oh, the Devil! I did not intend to preach a sermon. Tell me, what do you see as your goal in life?"

There was a hint of mischief in Truxton's voice and just the curl of a smile on his lips. "Well, Sir, since you ask I'd like your job."

Andrew chuckled, waving him out the door. "Get to your work! With that kind of posture, you might very well achieve it."

During the next two weeks, Truxton came to meet -- sometimes by formal introduction, sometimes by chance encounter -- the others in the growing ranks of the Young in Heart. There was Andrew, Jr., who had recently left college after several abortive attempts at higher education; and his cousin, Andrew Hutchings, whose studies seemed to be in similar disarray; and Daniel Donelson, who had attended West Point and achieved honors at the Military Academy, now in its 27th year. Another ward was Anthony Wayne Butler, who seemed always to be having difficulties with money. A frequent visitor, though not a permanent resident of the White House, was Samuel Jackson Hays, yet another nephew of the President.

I, of course, knew all these young people intimately since most had come from, or lived in, Nashville.

Then there was the young Indian boy, Lincoyer, now in his teens and quite a proper young gentleman. Sadly, he was confined much to his room with an ague that the physicians seemed unable to alleviate. His days were numbered and his death was to be a blow to Andrew when consumption took him from the family circle.

Truxton could scarce believe his good fortune when he discovered that the White House was the rendezvous for, if not the residence of, any number of winsome young ladies. He quickly had eyes for Mary Coffee, a pert and lively debutante of 18, only to find to his dismay that Andy Hutchings was a step ahead of him (*"She is so joyful, I view her as a treasure I"*) and was all but engaged.

Flora Hutchinson was equally engaging, with long, golden hair that seemed constantly in motion. Andrew, Jr. was particularly fond of her. Uncle Andrew, however, discouraged any serious attachment on the grounds that Flora, "though a fine little girl, is given to coquetry. I do not think a coquette would make a proper wife for a young man who himself is somewhat given to fickleness."

Still, there were plenty of other choices, including Rebecca McLane, Irish-born and with flaming red hair, Cora Livingstone, Peggy Branch, Mary McLemore, and one Mary Smith, who occasionally rode up from Alexandria.

The President found himself choked with embarrassment on one occasion because of the last-mentioned young lady. He had to admonish Andrew, Jr. (*who had finally found Flora too capricious*) for having discussed serious matters of the heart with Mary Smith without first having made his designs known to her parents.

"My nephew," he wrote to her father, Major Francis Smith, "has erred in attempting to address your daughter without first making known to you and your Lady his honorable intentions and obtaining your approbation.

Encouraging though the President was in attracting young people to the White House, he was by no means overindulgent. He hesitated not a whit to take to task any person whom he felt had stepped off the path of good taste or failed to discharge some social duty.

"Lazy Toads!" he scrawled in a bold hand on a memo to one unfortunate escort whose two female guests had failed to send thank-you notes after their stay.

He was constantly at odds, though in his deeply concerned and affectionate way, with Andrew, Jr., Anthony Butler, and Andy Hutchings. One or another of them was always in trouble for infractions of the rules, poor marks, or debts at the institutions of higher learning where they had been sent at considerable expense. He could be harsh and imposing in meeting these delinquencies head on. Yet he once confided in me that he knew how hard it was for young men to apply themselves when there were so many pleasurable distractions: sports, the lure of the gambling table, and, of course, the young ladies.

"I cannot censure them too harshly, Annie-Belle," he confessed, "since I found it hard to resist gaming when I was a youth, I was partial to horse racing, and my studies often were pushed into a corner when there were more lively entertainments afoot."

Andrew was a dupe though I think he knew it for the wiles of the young ladies who offered imaginative excuses for the likes of Andrew, Jr., Butler, and Hutchings when they fell out of grace. And he was an easy mark for Anne Royall, the only female journalist in Washington, who literally had the run of the White House and was the bane of male journalists who often found it frustrating to try to obtain some "inside" views from the President.

She told Andrew that his nephew, Andrew, Jr., was "sweetness and innocence itself, his eyes as soft as the dew drops." He succumbed instantly to this kind of sentiment, completely belying the opinions of writers and editors who often depicted him as a rough-shod old warrior, more at home on the battle-ground than in the parlor. He had many tender qualities. Anne's favorite story was the one about the lamb in the East Room.

She arrived for an appointment with the President one wet, chilly evening. But no one could find Andrew... not in his office or study or chambers. Miss Royall detected what seemed to be the bleat of a lamb and followed the sound to the East Room. There sat the President, before the fire, holding the little daughter of the housekeeper on one knee and the forepaws of a lamb on the other.

"What could I do?" he asked, "The child was upset because the animal was at the back door, wet and cold. The tears would not stop until I carried the lamb in.

"And here we are, warm and drying off."

Chapter 8

Becky Hayes arrived at the White House on a bright, windy day in early May, 1829.

It was a moment of great triumph for me. Andrew had asked a number of times about her "tragic circumstances" and dark future. Yet whenever I approached her about leaving Tennessee and moving to Washington, she had balked at the thought of abandoning her magnificent wilderness of mountains and trails and forests for the harsh bricks and stones and noisy crowds she pictured in this inhospitable city.

Finally, I had prevailed. But only because I myself was moving to Washington for a year or so to care for an older sister who lived there alone and had recently been crippled in a carriage accident.

"I promise you," I assured Becky, "that if you find the nation's capital unfriendly or otherwise distasteful, I shall personally conduct you back to Nashville within the month."

So it was that she packed her belongings tatty though some of them were in one of my aunt's hand-me-down carpetbags and accompanied me to Washington.

My moment of triumph almost ended at the White House door.

Unfortunately, one of the first people she met was Truxton Blair, who was conducting one of his firm's clients on a private tour of the building and grounds. He took an almost instant dislike to Becky, particularly upon learning that she had come, not for a visit but to stay.

"You cannot mean it, Annie-Belle," he whispered, having drawn me momentarily aside, "that Mr. Jackson has *invited* this girl? Why, she is as wild and disheveled as a bobcat."

"Oh, she is different, all right," I admitted in a hushed tone, "not like the gracious maidens you are accustomed to beating at whist in the music room."

"What's worse, she reeks of horseflesh. Perhaps she should be given a room in the stables!"

As ill luck would have it, his voice rose as he spoke, enough so that Becky caught the tail end of this conversation. By the time I got her away from the front hall and into the President's study, she was in tears.

Had it not been for Andrew's great gift for understanding and sympathizing with people, I would even then have been planning a return trip to Nashville. He made the girl feel welcome, dissolved the tears, and had us all in a good humor and ready for hot tea and corn cakes.

To Becky's eminent credit, I must say that she seemed as capable of weathering social storms in civilization as she did tempests in the wilderness. Although she was like a rough garnet compared with polished opals, she was quickly accepted by Mary Coffee, Cora Livinqstofle, Rebecca McLane, Peggy Branch, and Mary McLemore as one of the inner group. In fact, they enjoyed her tomboy antics, marveled at the control she had over the most fractious steed in the stable, and were captivated by the flinty inflections of her back-country idioms.

Above all, they were infected by the spirit of exuberance and adventure she brought to what for them had become almost routine: a never-ending exploration of the White House, the grounds, and the environs.

"I am so thankful Becky came along," said the red-haired Rebecca McLane. Here we all were, starting to take this place for granted and now she has shown us that we dwell in a palace like none ever found in the stories of The Thousand and One Nights."

The White House -- it was indeed an institution such as had never existed anywhere else in history.

After Andrew Jackson took up residence, there were really two "White Houses." The first was the private home of the man, replete with love and endearment and people. Barren of majestic trappings and luxurious embellishments, and still only partially furnished, it nevertheless offered the comforts of a private mansion like the Hermitage.

The second White House was the official structure that symbolized the material substance of the Presidency. As such, it was something of an embarrassment to American dignitaries in Washington who were constantly being visited by their counterparts from abroad. It suffered painfully by comparison with the great estates of the British monarchy, the chateaux maintained near Paris by members of the French delegation, or even the venerable manses of peripatetic Dutch burghers, who arched their bushy eyebrows at the nation's capital as being not nearly so "civilized" as Manhattan.

The White House grounds were pleasing, yet hardly elegant, reflecting the efforts of earlier occupants to enhance their temporary environment. Several strange mounds had been formed by one of Jefferson's gardeners in the rear yard. The walks were lined with some 20 American elms planted by John Quincy Adams, in company with scarlet oaks, white oaks, black walnuts and American boxwood. Jackson himself intended to add stands of magnolia grandiflora as soon as he could make arrangements to have them shipped north from the Hermitage.

During the past four years, John Quincy Adams, an avid gardener, had made numerous plantings, including herbs, vegetables, small fruit trees, shrubs, hedges, and flowers. He had also constructed several small hothouses which were lush with sage, tarragon, rue, white-flowered carrots, some medicinal herbs, and delicate flowers for his tables.

Most of the formal layouts were the work of Charles Bezat, who was appointed Gardener to the President during the Monroe administration. He designed a parterre garden in the French style in front of the West Pavilion, with loving attention to each detail.

Never having viewed a formal garden in her life, Becky Hays was captivated. "It is like a giant's quilt," she said to me when her eyes first glimpsed flowers of different shapes and sizes and colors formed into ornamental arrangements. One of her greatest pleasures was to sit on the grass, knees pulled up to her chin, and watch Mr. Bezat at work.

"What are those wine-red blossoms by the walk?" she would ask, or "Will those copper-colored buds have the same tint when they bloom?"

She was as much taken by his accent as by the explanations he gave and would frequently imitate his

Gallic enunciations when she and her companions were inside and came upon freshly filled vases.

Much of the White House was in turmoil, which may have been a happy situation in view of the foot-loose and not always tidy habits of the young vagabonds who occupied it. The South Portico had been completed five years earlier, but was undergoing a few alterations to conform to the North Portico, the scene of feverish construction. The great East Room was receiving its final touches, with most of the furniture protected by old blankets and pushed into corners.

The imported Bellange chairs purchased by the Monroes were worn and scuffed and badly needed restoration.

The exterior was still far from elegant, facing onto a 40-foot-wide strip of hard-packed clay known as Pennsylvania Avenue. In back, the area where a carriage house and stables were planned still contained nothing but a tottering barn and horse sheds that had been hastily built during the War of 1812. The East and West yards housed two squeaky iron pumps, the total source of the White House water supply. Brought in by pail, rather than pipes, the water was heated if desired on the wood stoves in the kitchen. The stately driveways and gravel walks (as they looked on paper) were muddy and without edging.

Much of the mud and clay found its way inside, leaving reddish stains on carpets and hardboard flooring.

As far as the smoky, fading color was concerned on the exterior woodwork and stone, the building would better have been referred to as the "Gray House."

One of Andrew's favorite diversions was to arise early in the morning (he did not sleep much anyway, because of his chronic insomnia) and walk down the tree-dotted South lawn to the Potomac River.

Since I was an early riser myself, I would often ride along the muddy banks when the day was fresh and the weather mild. If I saw Andrew coming, hobbling a little from old wounds and injuries, I would dismount and walk beside him for a few hundred yards. He enjoyed the company of an old friend. Sometimes we walked in silence, observing awakening nature around us. Occasionally he was talkative, taking the opportunity to flush out some of the concerns and frictions within him.

Around midsummer of that first year he was in the White House, I began noticing that fewer and fewer of our strolls were taken in silence. He seemed almost eager to unburden himself of despondencies and doubts. At first I attributed his dark mood to the climate and the season. Washington was notorious for its smothering Julys and Augusts, when the Potomac simmered in stillness and most residents -- at least the ones with any means -- escaped to retreats in the North.

Part of his depression stemmed, I knew, from the recent death of his Indian ward, Nicoyer. But the rest?

He was much pressed in matters at the Capitol. In one of the most sweeping decisions ever made by a President, he had all but scrapped his Cabinet and appointed new members to most of the positions.

"My enemies," he told me, "refer to my new cabinet as the 'Kitchen Cabinet,' inferring, I suppose, that the members are more suited to chores in the scullery than duties of state." He tried to make a joke of it, hut I saw more sobriety than humor on his countenance.

The opposition was so bitter that Andrew often felt he was being personally, as well as politically, attacked. He never got over the slap in the face from former President John Quincy Adams gave him by avoiding the inauguration ceremonies. Yet even his own constituents presented problems of equal magnitude. Washington swarmed with people who had supported him during the election and were now demanding sugarplum jobs under the customary "spoils system" that previous administrations had fostered.

There was little I could do about these tormenting political and administrative burdens, other than to offer heartfelt sympathy, as one friend to another. What really vexed me was that those of us who were close to him seemed to aggravate, rather than ameliorate, the problems. On at least three occasions recently, I had been the unwilling party to gossip that Truxton Blair was making life in the White House miserable for Becky Hayes. I had about decided to tongue-lash the young man at the earliest opportunity.

"I feel quite guilty, Sir," I confessed to Andrew during one of our early morning walks by the Potomac, "that I have not bestirred myself more often to the White House to teach these young people some manners.

"Why should you feel guilty?" His tone was chiding and not the least bit appreciative of my sentiment.

"I undertook -- and willingly -- to encourage both Truxton and Becky to move from Nashville to Washington. Yet I neglected to indoctrinate them in the rudiments of common courtesy, young to old and peer to peer.

"Why, Annie-Belle, I find all of my young people to be properly respectful." He held up his hickory walking stick and swirled it vigorously in the air as though trying to churn the morning mists. "You and I are getting older. We must not lose sight of the fact that the young tend, by natural instinct, to be over-spirited and contrary."

"True, Sir, yet enough is enough. There is no excuse for you to have to return to your chambers after troublesome confrontments with Congress to find a cat-and-dog fight in your own back yard."

"Cat-and-dog fight?"

"I refer singularly to Truxton and Becky, Sir. The snarling and baring of claws must surely be disconcerting to you when you hope for moments of contemplation and relaxation."

Andrew wedged the walking stick up under his arm, took both my hands in his with great warmth and looked me straight in the eyes. He laughed loudly, but this time with heartiness and levity, "Nay, nay. I find their heated give and take buoyant to my spirit, refreshment to the soul.

"I would as soon discourage their romantic skirmishing as I would hobble colts and fillies gallivanting in the pasture. The sight of true love in its first blush is a great joy to me... "

"But surely, you cannot believe that Becky and Truxton are in *love*!"

"I can and I do." He dropped my hands and continued his stroll, "I am surprised at you, Annie-Belle, if you do not recognize the sorcery taking place -- you who have had a dozen lovers in your day, and perhaps still do."

"You have been closer, Sir, to the situation I do believe, or else my vision is becoming cloudy."

"Perhaps, perhaps. Neither Miss Hayes nor Mr. Blair is the drawing-room type of sweetheart. The course of their love will never run smooth. Rather, it will be like a stream in the Blue Ridge, tumbling and turning, leaping and hurtling over the rocks."

Andrew Jackson paused and looked upward and outward over the Potomac, as though trying to pierce the morning mists with his steel blue eyes and see beyond this veil of life. For a minute or two he was as completely lost in his thoughts as though I had been a thousand miles away and the city of Washington but a vapor. I knew he was thinking of Rachel -- the Rachel he had known and courted at the age of 23 when I was infatuated with him and crushed at the thought that he had eyes only for some one else.

Becky reminded him of Rachel Donelson, with the jet black hair that she sometimes let cascade over her shoulders, sometimes braided, Indian-style, when she wanted to gallop wantonly bareback across the sweeping pastures. She was just as much the coquette, with an innate sense of mischief that could drive her peers to distraction. She was conspicuously the tomboy, yet sensuous enough so that her sex could never be mistaken. Her face had a dark beauty, with lips a little too wide, the small breasts of a Classic Greek statue, hips that were full, and legs that were long and well sculptured.

Andrew Jackson was, of course, vicariously in love with Becky, the reincarnation of the only woman who had ever shared his heart.

Was it wishful thinking when he pictured Becky and Truxton as lovers-to-be?

I thought about this possibility long after I had bid him good day that morning, remounted my horse, and cantered back to my sister's home. There were tiny clues here and there that he saw in Truxton Blair something of an embodiment of his own youth. Blair had many of the characteristics of Andrew as a young man: that chin-jutting pugnaciousness, an eagerness to single out adversaries to challenge, a compulsion to speak bluntly and with great conviction, an attraction for controversy and confrontation.

Truxton, like Andrew, was volatile and emotional, able to feed the fires of temperament, though at the same time possessing an inscrutable control over them.

Yes, I decided, Andrew Jackson was living a strange fantasy, entering a mystical world where the past was once again alive. To maintain this deeply emotional illusion, Truxton and Becky had to be on the verge of falling in love

Over the next few weeks, I made it a point to be at the White House more frequently, as unobtrusively as possible, so that I could observe what was transpiring and see how Andrew Jackson was faring. I had justification for my presence since the official housekeeper was ailing and it was not unwonted for me to volunteer to assist. I was alarmed to note very quickly that Andrew was coping with undercurrents of melancholy that sometimes surfaced but usually ran deep. In unguarded moments, I heard him mutter that "the people on the Hill" were out to discredit him. Henry Clay, in particular, and certain members of Congress were aiming barbs at his family life.

"They find fault in any absence I have from affairs of state. Clay even went so far as to use the phrase 'derelict in his duty' attributing it to a preoccupation with the personal pursuits of my young people.

"Do they fail to see that it is the young who will soon be shaping the very fortunes of this republic?"

Clay had already made a number of sniffling comments about Andrew, Jr., Andy Hutchings, and Anthony Butler when he found out that they had received poor marks and run up inexcusable debts at college. Now he was beginning to turn his attentions to Truxton Blair, who had a fine knack for stirring up controversy.

Truxton was a bear for work, leaving the White House every morning at dawn and trudging several blocks to his firm's office on New York Avenue, and seldom returning until after dusk. Because of his inquisitive and probing turn of mind his proximity to the nation's legislative halls, it was inevitable that he would enter the political stage -- or at least venture into the wings. It did not alleviate the sensitivities when Truxton took a strong dislike to Henry Clay.

"His oratory may be as smooth as the tones of a Church organ," he said bluntly to one Senator who had just been extolling the virtues of the gentleman from Kentucky, "but it is similarly made up of wind."

The utterance, of course, was made known to Clay who was more gratified than aggravated. After all, it provided him with a vulnerable target in his attacks on his arch enemy, Andrew Jackson. He could hamstring Jackson by cutting down his confederate, a young man obviously too politically naive and inexperienced to trade blows with a Congressional veteran.

Truxton's greatest trump was the fact that he did not know the strategy of withdrawal. Instead of retreating out of range of the political fusiliers, he strode right into their ranks so that they were afraid of shooting for fear of hitting each other. He discovered the <u>Feuilleton</u>, a most popular section of newspapers and periodicals that was devoted to critical comments from readers. Since young Blair was talented with the pen and had an eye for those subjects with the most nettles, his compositions were welcomed and encouraged by the editors.

On at least one occasion his comments were barbed enough so that there was talk of a duel, in defense of the "injured" politician's honor.

"The challenge died aborning," chuckled one <u>Feuilleton</u> editor, "when the subject of Mr. Blair's invective privately inquired about the skills of his intended adversary." It was confidentially revealed that the young barrister was well schooled in the use of the pistol. He was also an accomplished swordsman, surprisingly quick on his feet despite his deformity, alert, and deft with his hands, whether brandishing foil, épée, or saber.

When the maligned politician learned that even Blair's German fencing master had been bested by his pupil, he dropped all thought of a challenge and wrote a lame reply to the <u>Feuilleton</u> instead.

Truxton was not physically imposing. Standing at but five feet, eight inches (barely an inch taller than Becky), he was husky, with stocky shoulders. Coming from a family of means, he was invariably well tailored. He looked especially fitting -- even dashing -- in a military uniform. Although his lame foot kept him from active service, he still retained a commission in the Tennessee militia and was authorized to wear rank and colors on formal occasions until reaching his twenty-second year.

I always saw two personalities in Truxton: on the one side of the coin the volatile, emotional, passionate man of action; on the other, the refined, punctilious, often fastidious gentleman. Andrew Jackson's impressions were similar.

"They are good qualities for a man in the legal calling," he once commented." An attorney needs to be as careful and precise as a diamond-cutter and as unrattled as a tightrope walker. Yet he must also know how to put the devil's fire in his voice on occasion or the widow's tear in his eye.

I was deeply thankful for Truxton's presence in the White House and for his increasing agitations on the political scene. His communications and actions kept the President diverted from his incertitudes and seemed to dispel the vapors of his melancholy. Andrew savored a good fight as much as he ever had in the past, so he derived great pleasure -- if sometimes vicariously -- from the constant challenges Truxton was dealing with.

I do not mean only those that related to the practice of law, politics, or the governmental affairs of the young Republic. I am thinking -- perhaps even more so -- of the tempest-tossed love affair between Truxton Blair and Becky Hayes. At times, it seemed as though they had brought right into the White House with them a reincarnation of the great storm that had made the Cumberlands quake that night in Tennessee when they both were born.

Chapter 9

In all of Washington, from the Anacostia to the upper reaches of the Potomac, there could not have been two people of more dissimilar mien and temperament.

Where Truxton was natty of dress and carefully groomed, Becky favored loose-fitting homespuns and colorful ginghams that looked as though they had spent the previous week in variations of wind, sun, and rain. Where Truxton preferred the court, the club, and the drawing room, Becky was most buoyant when galloping across the countryside, splashing gloriously through Rock Creek, and coming to rest only when her mount was flecked with foam and whinnying for the stable.

In the matter of conversation, they were almost as far apart as the first and last pages of the dictionary. Truxton plunged into the most sober-sided topics, earnestly favoring the functions of government, controversial national issues, international affairs, and the policies and personalities of high-ranking officials. He supported, both verbally and fundamentally, the President's campaign to "extinguish the national debt and counteract the tendency to public profligacy."

He was outspoken in urging reform and the removal from Federal office of all who were incompetent or did not have the Republic's future uppermost in mind. He freely voiced his opinions of Henry Clay (negative), Martin Van Buren (positive), and vice president John Calhoun (in between). He had words, both kind and unkind, about states' rights. On the sensitive subject of Indian affairs, he was not nearly as paternal as the President and did not hesitate to tell Andrew to his face that he was coddling many who were little more than savages at heart."

As for Becky, she dwelt in a rare, sometimes fanciful conversational world that was shared in essence by few others -- whether peers or elders. She was not at all conversant with those issues relating to the government or events abroad, other than actions relating to the Indians, with whom she sided totally and unequivocally.

Besides the topics that seemed to interest Becky and Truxton separately, another great dissimilarity lay in their senses of humor. Sober though he was in conversations, the young man did have a considerable wit. Largely, it was expressed with an objective: to make a point in court, to take the air out of the sails of an opponent, to deride some issue that he found objectionable.

Becky's outlook on humor was much more light-hearted, though sometimes provocative. She loved to tease. She well deserved a term some of her elders tagged her with, "That little rapscallion!" She was sometimes a scalawag, a mischief maker with a penchant for practical jokes and salty comments. Nevertheless, the other young ladies at the White House doted on her knavery -- as long as they were not the butt of the joke.

Though much older (by now, *56*) I was occasionally the target of her whimsy. To me, it seemed more capricious -- perhaps even kittenish -- than it did to her impressionable peers.

"Fah! Annie-Belle," she said to me one day, "I can always get a reaction from Flora or Daniel or Peggy -- and sometimes from the President. But you do not always appreciate my little comedies."

"Oh, I do. I do," I protested, "My face may not reflect the joy I get from your amusements. I would rather hear happiness in your voice than in that of any one else I know.

"Except Andrew's... the President's."

"Indeed," she said, her tone abruptly serious, "He has been so melancholy these past weeks. I always pay him a compliment and display a cheerful mien when I am in his presence. Do you think that the burdens of state are heavier than anticipated? Or that his physical ailments --

he has more than any man I know of! -- are undermining his resolve?"

"Burdens perhaps, ailments no. He shakes off aches and pains and vapors as though they were so many fluttering moths in his face. I tell you frankly, Becky, that we are the cause of his mental dyspepsia."

"We? You and I and "Indirectly, I should say. He has such an overpowering paternal instinct -- maternal, too, perhaps -- that all of us who are part of his White House 'family' are as vital a part of his life as his Cabinet, his Congress, and the People who have continually voiced support. That kind of affection exasperates, and sometimes enrages, his opponents. Particularly men like Henry Clay and..."

"But I thought Mr. Clay to be a family man himself, with a brood of eleven children. Is that not so?"

"So true that it fuels his ire. He has so little concern about his own children, leaving their upbringing almost entirely in the hands of his wife, that he cannot stomach the idea of the President showing so much endearment for young people who are not even his own flesh and blood."

"And why should this person, Clay, *care* how the President distributes personal affections? Why indeed should he have any right to intrude?"

"Heed this well," I urged, holding up my forefinger like a preacher in the pulpit about to expose a hidden sin, "You have found the pebble in the boot. Not only a right but a *duty*, says Mr. Clay. Though he speaks without portfolio, he considers himself a watchdog, as the former secretary of state, to monitor the performances of men in high office.

"Still, how can he reproach Mr. Jackson, whose lamp usually flickers at his desk until far into the night?"

"Only in one way, really. He voices the premise -- which none can deny -- that the President devotes much time and personal concern to the increasing numbers of young people living in the White House. 'Ergo,' he expounds, every hour that the Chief of State devotes to these green saplings is one hour less that he devote to shoring up the seasoned timbers of state."

"I am not sure that I have his figures of speech quite right, but he constantly orates along similar lines."

A pall of gloom descended on Becky. She was seldom words moody, but I could see that my/held darker connotations than I had intended. Her first reaction was to suggest that we all leave the President more to himself and resolve to frequent those parts of the White House that he seldom visited.

"Oh, no!" I exclaimed with alarm, "you must not do that. You young people are more nourishment to him than the food on his table. Without you around, he would suffer an emotional starvation that would be mortal."

I was able to persuade her that this was so and that, if anything, she and the others should pay more -- rather than less -- attention to providing close companionship of the kind Andrew Jackson sorely needed.

If the President had favorites within the household, he certainly was most clever at disguising his opinions. That was not difficult, however, for he always threw himself earnestly into conversations, no matter who was engaging his attention. It continued to surprise me, for instance, that he was as equally at home with the nature topics favored by Becky as he was with the more weighty issues raised by Truxton. He could converse with either of them for an hour or more without once wavering in his interest.

"To tell truth," he commented to me one evening, "though I am intrigued by Blair's conspectus for stitching our torn relationships with Mexico, I am equally enthralled by Miss Hayes's forecasting. Did you know that she can predict rain by watching the curl on a willow leaf? An old Chickasaw knack."

Andrew was captivated by any circumstance that taught him something new or enlarged his knowledge about a subject with which he was already familiar.

Truxton opened the door to fresh insights on old problems. Becky brought closer to him the wonders of nature he had always been close to yet failed to observe.

He was equally delighted with any opportunity to teach other people, and did so with zest and vigor. When Becky arrived at the White House, she could barely write her own name and had no idea how to spell "Washington." Now, through Andrew's encouragement and the tutelage of red-haired Rebecca McLane, she was memorizing page after page from the <u>Virginia</u> <u>Reader</u> and practicing letter-writing -- by addressing longer and longer notes to me and others who knew her well and would not laugh at grammatical blunders or awkward phrasing.

Gripped in the humid fever of the long summer, life in Washington proceeded at a wearisome pace and there was not much to report about the affairs and fortunes of the young in heart. I was away much of the time, back in Nashville with my aunt. My first visit to the White House in more than two months came late in September of that year, 1829. Andrew seemed glad to see me and devoted the better part of an hour to a conversation in his study.

"Not much has happened, Annie-Belle, that is visible to the eye," he reported. As you must have noticed, the North Portico is now completed, except for some minor imperfections that are being remedied. And I am told that there is a new stove in the kitchen, one that will burn lump coal.

"My interest does not lie in the architecture, Sir," I blurted, my voice tremulous with curiosity, "What about the *people*? Becky and Truxton? And Rebecca, Cora, Andrew, Jr., Anthony, the three Marys, and the others? There was not a soul in sight when I walked down the corridor."

"They are all at the Old Mall," he explained, "recruiting volunteers and collecting funds for a new orphanage being built in Alexandria. It was young Blair's idea, since he and Becky and several of the others are orphans themselves. Most commendable."

The President was about to warm up to the subject of young people left alone in the world - one of his favorite topics - and I could see that we might be into it for the duration of our intercourse if I did not quickly switch the conversation to what was uppermost in my thoughts.

"What a worthy venture!" I exclaimed loudly and abruptly enough to dislodge him from his thoughts, "and so like Truxton Blair to come up with the idea. But tell me, Sir, how is he faring these days in the courts of law ? And what of Becky and her lessons?"

He provided much the kind of information I expected: that Truxton was rapidly making a name for himself as a barrister; that his appetite for political stew had not diminished; and that Becky could now write a page or more of composition, "with no more errors than you or I might inflict on the tablet."

"Good, good. I see that they are progressing well in their secular objectives. But what of romance? Have you had reason to reconsider your earlier impression that there was a sentiment budding?"

I fully expected him to shake his head sadly and admit that he had been guilty of a flight of fancy. But no. He suddenly clapped his thin hands together with a sound like a pistol shot and leaned forward across the scarred old desk. His blue eyes danced.

"Quite the contrary, dear lady! I know young love aborning when I see the signs. And this has been no exception. They may not know the truth yet -- as they imitate the dog and cat -- but I have been observant, which as you know is my nature.

"True, sir. There is not much that misses your eye."

"And I can tell you that these two are destined to be lovers. Would you enjoy a brief lesson in the art of divining?"

"I would indeed," I replied with unabashed enthusiasm, "if it pleases you to continue."

"Young Truxton makes a great show of turning up his nose when he is in the company of other young people and Becky enters the room. This tells me that he is secretly attracted to her, but cannot resolve the thought that he was to the manor born and she to a settler's cabin.

"He enjoys well the companionship of the misses Coffee, Branch, McLane, and the other young ladies who are well schooled in the social graces and attractive partners for the dance, croquet, or a game of whist. Yet while he is enjoying such conventional pursuits, I note that his ears open and his nose gives a little twitch whenever some one mentions Becky and her latest escapades and pranks.

"He is quite responsive to the attentions of Rebecca McLane -- as who would not be? C yet he makes particular ado about her when Becky is in the room. It is evident to me (if not to young Blair) that this is a deceit to enhance his desirability in the eyes of the one he really loves.

"Ahh, Annie-Belle, I could delineate many other observations. But do not these few suggest something of a romantic nature to you?"

"They do indeed. Now tell me abut Becky Hayes. What divinations and portents relate to her?"

The conversation reminded me of the time I had visited a practitioner of ceromancy, who had predicted the outcome of one of my own love affairs by dropping melted wax into cold water and studying the patterns that formed on the surface. Not until later, though, did it strike me as being incongruous that I should be listening to the President of the Republic as he earnestly and cleverly played the role of clairvoyant.

"Becky? It would take a veritable soothsayer to unlock the secrets of that radiant child's head and heart. Still, do not fear, I have done so to my full satisfaction. And I think to yours.

"She is very open-faced in her emotions and reactions. I can observe her as she sips punch in the garden with young Donelson and Butler and see that her expressions and reactions are much less sophisticated and self-conscious than those of the other young ladies. She does not play cards with her emotions, but is quite natural."

"And when she is with Truxton?"

"The same. She lets her thoughts come to the surface. It is amusing to watch her, out of the corner of my good eye, of course. If she thinks that her beloved is shielding his emotions or being too urbane or genteel, she berates him, affectionately, and tells him to discard the actor's role."

"How does he respond?"

"Not well at all. He becomes confused and tends to retreat. The problem right now is that he does not yet know that he is in love."

"Perhaps he is more attracted to some one who is more clever, socially, than Becky. Like Rebecca McLane."

"That is the way it seems. But only on the surface."

The President described an event that had taken place in late September, while I was still away: the formal dedication of the North Portico. All of the Cabinet members of the former administration had been invited (since the plans were laid during the Adams Presidency). Of the few who attended, the most conspicuous was Henry Clay, who had served as Secretary of State.

"I did not expect the man to have the impudence to set foot on my doorstep," muttered the President, "but he walked in, smiling and bowing, and immediately ingratiating himself with the young people. He used his wit and congeniality -- as you know how well he can do -- to make me look the fool for ever saying unkind words about him."

"I thought he had retired and was permanently out of Washington.

"Oh yes, he did play the Kentucky gentleman for awhile as master of his great plantation at Ashland. But back he has been itching to get into politics. Failing that, he must perpetually be sticking his nose into the business of other people.

"He had the gall to question my own staff members, as though he were some special emissary of the people -- an investigator, to put it bluntly."

"He questioned them? About what?"

"Life at the White House. Activities. Amusements and divertissements. All the time probing and prying, like a spy. His intention -- plain as a pikestaff -- was to determine the nature of my daily schedule and the scope of my activities."

"So much the better, Sir. Then he must have learned that you do not spend your time gambling, cock-fighting, racing horses, and otherwise idling away your time -- as some of your detractors would have the public believe.

"No, but his very presence is baneful news for me. He will tickle the ears of his drones with descriptions of me as the paternal uncle, the coddler of children, the household busybody, ever puttering. That sinister strategy, 'to damn with faint praise,' is one of his most well honed weapons.

Without warning, he suddenly brought both spindly fists down hard on the desk top with a sound like a log being split.

"Damnation! Damnation!" he barked. "You see what I mean? That villain -- just thinking about him -- has deflected my thoughts from their intended course. I had it in mind to give you my observations about budding love."

He promptly recovered himself, as was his wont, and lost himself in an account of Becky and Truxton during the course of the dedication festivities.

"The chase was much in evidence," he mused, savoring each recollection, "and though I was much monopolized by legislators and others utilizing this opportunity to gain my ear, I was surprisingly observant. I could see that Mistress McLane was pursuing barrister Blair persistently and adroitly.

"Was he enjoying the chase?"

"Yes, yes, Annie-Belle, except for one distraction:

He could plainly see that Mistress Hayes was being equally courted by esquire Hutchings. And with no displeasure on her part."

"The picture is quite clear. To quote the poet (though I may not be accurate), 'If jealousy creeps in, can love be far behind?' Did Becky seem tweaked by Rebecca's attentions to Truxton?"

"Not to my notice. Not to her notice either, I think I can state with impunity. She is too much a child of nature. Any dismay would immediately have clouded her features.

My conversation with Andrew that day left me disquieted, harshly in contrast to his almost smug conviction that the love affair would see fruition. Now I was exceedingly concerned about Becky. Although she could be coquettish and flirtatious, her style was kittenish and no match for the feline wiles of the red-haired Rebecca McLane.

The latter made it a point to know politics, read the law journals, and know where legislators stood on important issues. With that kind of lubricant for her tongue, she could talk Truxton's language freely, flatter him skillfully about his accomplishments, and make Becky Hayes seem like a mute by comparison.

The presence of Henry Clay worried me considerably, as it did the President, though for a different reason. If Clay were to aim his barbs at Truxton as a means of baiting the President, Rebecca could supply sympathy and understanding. And Becky? She would be dumbfounded and confused, much as Rachel had been when Andrew Jackson was campaigning for the Presidency and his opponents resorted to the most malicious sort of slander.

No, Becky Hayes would have been lost to Truxton's forever had it not been for witchcraft on All Soul's Eve and a near-tragic event that occurred some four weeks later.

Chapter 10

"A birthday party -- that's what we must have!"

I could scarce believe it when Andrew Jackson announced during the first week in October that he was going to plan and host a joint event for Becky Hays and Truxton Blair on All Soul's Eve. Yet I should have known that such an idea would spark his imagination and kindle his romantic heart. He was captivated, too, by events that smacked of witchcraft and the occult.

What better on that ghostly evening than to commemorate two births that took place when thunder shook the hills and sabers of lightning pierced the clouds!

It was not difficult for me to predict the reactions of the two principals who were to be so singularly honored.

"What an exciting idea," exclaimed Becky to her chamber mates, "The President does not know it, but I am the descendent of a Chickasaw ghost who will materialize promptly on the stroke of midnight -- in full headdress, and with a bow three feet long, carved from the topmost limb of a giant yaw-yaw tree."

"He will let loose a single arrow, which will blaze with light in its flight and head skyward until it pierces the moon."

"The devil you say!" rumbled Truxton when he first heard about the President's plan, "I just hope Mr. Clay never gets wind of this, or he'll ride his own broomstick right into the Halls of Congress and make us all out to be puerile or senile, as the case may be."

Nonetheless, he conditioned himself stoically for the night of October 31, 1829, knowing that when Andrew Jackson made a decision it was as hard to eradicate as an oak stump.

To tell the truth, I found myself tingling with anticipation and intoxicated by the whole idea. Daily, right up until the very morning of the event, the White House staff, such as it was, received scribbles and scrawls from the President on whatever bits of paper were handy.

He was continually having ideas relating to the refreshments, the music to be played, the dance numbers, and a host of prizes that would be given out: for costumes, wigs, make-up, terpsichorean skills, and so on and on.

Some 50 young people responded to the invitation to the Bal Masque on Hallow's Eve, scheduled, as the description read, "to begin when the daylight has receded enough so the Ghosts and Hobgoblings are ready to leave their nether abodes and appear in the presence of mortals." The evening was still, with just enough breeze to shake the jack-o'-lanterns strung throughout the White House gardens and make their candles flicker eerily. The autumn sky was clear, but paraded with clouds whose ever--changing sizes and shapes transformed them from cattle and birds and sailing ships to gnomes and trees - and of course witches.

All around Washington, as was the custom, bonfires blazed at every location where townspeople gathered, and whale oil lamps flickered in the graveyards, providing just enough light to discourage underworld demons from appearing to cast spells upon the families of the departed.

The masquerade ball was preceded by fortune-telling, for any guests plucky enough to venture into a dim, tiny anteroom just off the East Room where the dancing was to take place. For some, the sight of the wrinkled crone who huddled behind a glowing crystal ball was less frightening than the dire predictions that cackled from her snag-toothed mouth.

"It is all in fun," explained Becky to one young maiden of no more than 15 who emerged shaken and in tears, "you did not hear the voice of a witch but only that of

Potele, the pastry cook, who lines her face with charcoal and wears a hideous horsehair periwig."

Mummers and mimes were much in evidence, prancing the hallways from one end of the mansion to the other, sometimes bowing, sometimes mocking the guests.

There was much clapping when the President himself appeared briefly to usher in the members of the orchestra, dressed in such ghostly costumes that they must have startled many a passerby en route to the White House. Within moments, the masquerade ball, the joint birthday celebration, would be under way.

When I first saw Becky Hayes that evening, I could not stifle a gasp. She was striking. All of the other young ladies wore wigs, some quite elaborate. She alone did not. Instead, she had skillfully and cleverly braided her dark, dark hair so that it ran down the sides of her face and around her white throat like a necklace of unusual proportions. She was a portrait in an ebony frame.

All of the other young ladies wore petit silk masks over their eyes, some bejeweled, and rubbings of chalk rouge on their cheeks. But Becky, she had turned back to the Chickasaw strain in her heritage, making her "mask" out of berry juices that stained her cheek bones and hollows of her eyes. "It is an ancient custom," she explained to me when I complimented her on her unique skill. "Indian maidens who reach the age of 16 are said to 'come into flower' and are decorated accordingly. Though this is my twentieth birthday, it is the first celebration I have ever had. So I must make the best of the opportunity."

She did not try to carry this theme into her dress, and wisely so I thought. Instead, she wore a wine-red velvet gown, traditional in style, but pinched slightly at the top to enhance her bosom and tight at the hips where her natural lines needed no seamstress's assistance to make them appealing to the eye.

Even as I marveled at Becky's provocative beauty, I was struck by a twinge of doubt. Here she was -- perhaps deliberately -- emphasizing the one characteristic that Truxton had most demeaned: her "savage" heritage.

"We have a little savage in our midst," he had re-marked but a few weeks earlier, while watching Becky urging her high-mettled mustang over a series of difficult jumps, "If we are not careful, she may come after our scalps!"

What would his reaction be now?

My only hope was that perhaps some of the President's judgment had rubbed off on Truxton. Andrew, contrarily, was outspoken in his admiration of Becky and her devotion to her lineage. He respected her native imagination and lack of social embarrassment, despite her very humble, unfortunate, and secretive birth. After all, he himself had sprung from obscure origins - yet was as proud of his frontier ancestry as she was.

He did not hesitate to make his opinions known to Truxton, bluntly, whenever the occasion warranted it.

The moment of truth came a few minutes after the spectral orchestra had struck up its first tune, a stately minuet, to get the guests in a mood for dancing.

I was seated in a corner of the East Room, next to the doorway leading into the front corridor, where I had been stationed by the President to check off the names of guests as they arrived. Becky was not 20 feet away, in spirited conversation with Flora Hutchinson, who was not unlike her in stature and the dark set of her hair. At that moment, clear across the freshly waxed dance floor, Truxton Blair appeared on the scene. In black robes and a white, powdered wig, he was costumed as a judge. He so looked the part that I caught my breath momentarily, wondering whether perhaps he had received a judicial appointment of which I was unaware.

The realization came to me immediately thereafter: If the president were going to insist on making his wards masquerade, then - by God! - he, Truxton, was going to seize the opportunity to demonstrate that he looked the part to which he aspired in real life.

He strode directly across the room, yet without noticing Becky since his gaze was on Rebecca McLane, who stood fanning herself with consummate poise just beyond where I sat. Of a sudden, his gaze was distracted by the dark beauty and dramatic artistry of mistress Hayes. I could not miss the impulsive glint that lit his features. He veered in his course and headed her way, as though to engage her in conversation.

With equal abruptness, he stopped in mid-stride. I could almost hear him exclaim, "The devil! It's that cursed Hayes girl - *not* a lovely stranger!"

But now she had noticed him and smiled in recognition -- and I am afraid in anticipation. Flustered, with face reddening, in contrast to the absolute whiteness of the wig, he half tripped, wavered, and changed course back towards Rebecca McLane. I could tell how unnerved he was by the way he involuntarily gripped the folds of his robe with tight hands.

Becky's smile dissolved. I was flushed with sympathy for her and infuriated at Truxton's snub. I felt an urge to slap his cheek and reprove him for acting like an urchin.

"Judge of the court, indeed I" I would reprimand him, "better that you come dressed as a bumpkin!"

I was diverted -- fortunately for all concerned -- by the arrival of some latecomers, and for the next ten minutes was occupied with playing the hostess. By then it was almost time for the Grand Promenade, a formal procession around the perimeter of the East Room so that the young guests might properly be presented to the President and the elders serving as hosts and hostesses. Ironically, the Promenade was to be led by Becky and Truxton, hand in arm, unanimously selected for the honor as the birthday celebrants.

After a suitable fanfare by the orchestra and the expected confusion as partners sought each other and lined up in their appointed positions, the Promenade commenced.

What was in Truxton's mind, I wondered, as he and Becky stepped forward in unison, aware of the curious contrast between the dignified (*stuffy might be a better term*) judge and the ebony-dressed maiden in war paint.

Truxton's reaction was interesting for me to behold. Stiff and cavalier at first, his demeanor softened and became more respectful as he came to realize how many masculine eyes were drawn to his partner. When they passed the Presidential chair, with its Seal of State, Andrew rose ebulliently from his seat, bowed low to Becky and kissed her hand. The glint in his eye reflected both affection and pride.

That one look marked a turning point.

Although Truxton paid much attention to the other young ladies, particularly Rebecca and Flora, I was pleased, and surprised, to see him invite Becky as his partner for the quadrille, an elaborate and stately series of steps that displayed her grace and skill to the fullest. Later, he also selected her for two waltzes, a sprightly gavotte, and a cotillion.

The President retired early, not because he was fatigued and heading for bed. Rather, he felt that the young should be left to themselves as much as possible on such an occasion. He went so far as to shock several elders by suggesting that they all retire, too, at least from the East Room and vicinity. There were refreshments and a couple of fiddlers for the older guests, he said, if they would betake themselves downstairs one flight to the oval Diplomatic Room.

"Why he is as much as urging us to leave our sons and daughters un-chaperoned!" exclaimed one Virginia matron who considered such a situation tantamount to approving Original Sin.

Those of us of a more romantic turn of mind, including the President, were little worried -- not even when harpsichord, flutes, dulcimers, and violins were silenced and those of the guests who remained filtered outside. There, in the sentimental glow of jack-o'-lanterns and flickering candles, they strolled through the gardens or bobbed for apples. Several clever young men told ghost stories in hollow voices, with the intention of making their sweethearts cuddle closer for protection.

Did Becky and Truxton end the evening together, drawn by the magnetism that was earlier apparent? Although I tactfully tried to draw some gossip from their peers during the next few days, my efforts were futile. Apparently Becky had retired to her chambers after an hour or so in the garden, her bodice soaked and her face smeared from bobbing for apples. Truxton? He was seen a few times in earnest conversation with Rebecca.

"Probably talking politics," huffed Flora, miffed that she had received too little attention from Blair, "She's a nimble one with her tongue and can keep Truxton at her side as deftly as she holds her horse to tether."

The situation looked bleak.

I was depressed.

"Get hold of yourself, Annie-Belle," I scolded myself, "Why should you care whether Truxton married Becky or Rebecca -- or some maiden named Louisa whom he has not yet met?" But I *did* care. And I could see the romance dying before it ever had a chance to flower.

It might have, too, had it not been for Andrew Jackson's unexpected decision to proclaim Thanksgiving.

"Thanksgiving?" I said to Andrew when he told me his plan, and showing my embarrassment at being so ignorant about an event that obviously was dear to his heart.

"Yes, yes. It was first observed by President Washington on November 26, 1879, during his first year in office. No one has really given much thought to the occasion since.

"We have much to be thankful for, as a nation. The early settlers recognized that when their plantings survived and the autumn harvest was good. I should like to see Thanksgiving become a national holiday at the end of each November. As you well know, I am not a particularly religious man - my profanity alone deters preachers from seeking my attendance at worship - but I do feel that we should be more thankful for our many blessings...

"And, therefore ..."

"Therefore, I am proclaiming that we shall observe Thanksgiving this year. At least in the White House and in Washington at large."

So it was that on the last Thursday in November, almost four weeks after the masquerade ball, we assembled around a huge, makeshift table in the unfinished ball that was to be the State Dining Room. There were twenty of us that noon, including seven of us who were elders and fourteen of the Young in Heart. Andrew intoned the blessing, reading from a Proclamation he had printed and submitted to Congress.

The afternoon was cool and crisp, just what was needed to clear our heads after many courses and a round of fine wines. Brisk walks were popular, until several of the more adventuresome suggested informal horse races across the meadows. Becky, for one, was quick to respond and in no time at all had successfully challenged and beaten not only two of the young ladies, but Anthony Butler as well.

Truxton, who at first had dismissed Becky's challenge with indifference, now did an about face, determined that she should have her comeuppance.

"That conceited little filly," he said to Andy Hutchings, "I'll give her a head start and beat her by a furlong.

"And I hope her mount balks and she falls on her face."

Ten minutes later, he was choking on his wish. An outstanding horseman, he was much more of a match for Becky than Butler and was leading by a good fifty meters. Ahead of him at the hastily marked finish line, he could see his friends waving, laughing and cheering him on.

Of a sudden, he saw the laughter vanish, replaced by looks of alarm. Turning his head while still at the gallop, he saw Becky's mustang down and the girl sprawled on the grass.

He reined to a halt and trotted quickly back in her direction. He was overcome with horror as he saw Becky's form, totally limp on the ground, her dark hair swirled eerily over her face, her riding crop and scarf strewn across the turf. The position of her head terrified him.

"She has broken her neck!" he shouted back towards the others.

I was astride my own horse, on the sidelines and the nearest one to the accident. Truxton's words struck me like a dagger. He all but plunged from his horse and rushed to Becky's side, putting his ear to her breast to listen for a heartbeat.

Then the most wondrous act took place. He put his lips to hers and kissed her in an impetuous, impulsive testimony of love. The others did not see his actions -- they were still too far away and partially shielded from view by his horse. But I saw everything clearly. I saw Becky stir slightly, watched Truxton tilt back and away from her, with a look of consternation over what he had just done, and heard him entreating her to say that she was all right.

By the time I reached them and had dismounted to render assistance, Becky was sitting up and rubbing her neck gingerly with both hands.

"Lie down, please," I cautioned, "until we examine you. If there are any broken bones, you will simply aggravate the injuries.

"I am fine, Annie-Belle," she protested, "except for a little breath knocked out of my lungs. Anyway, I deserved to end up in the mud. I was watching my competitor instead of the turf and went right into a sink hole."

Had I not been so concerned lest Becky had some hidden injury, I should have been amused at the reactions of Truxton Blair. Realizing that he had revealed his innermost emotions -- to himself as well as to me -- he looked as embarrassed as a guest who has just tipped over the wine bottle on the hostess's white table cloth. His face alternated between strawberry red and ashen white.

Worst of all, he did not know whether Becky had regained consciousness in time to feel the stolen kiss on her lips.

We summoned a carriage and transported our fallen champion across the fields to the White House. Within the hour, Andrew's physician had pronounced her quite fit, suffering only from what he referred to as "a pulled neck."

It was Truxton who had received the greatest, and most permanent wound: an arrow straight to his heart.

Oh that wonderful, that magic kiss I could not wait to tell Andrew Jackson about it and see the look of jubilation on his face.

Chapter 11

I should not have laughed at Truxton's discomposure, for he suffered dolours of the heart that were truly akin to physical maladies and agues. He had that faraway look of one who is in fever and cannot assemble his thoughts clearly. He fidgeted and fussed like a person with stomach distress. He coughed and cleared his throat whenever some one engaged him unexpectedly in conversation, as though he were in the first stages of consumption.

Most noticeably -- at least to me -- he had a compulsion to remove himself from our society as often as possible during the next few days, like the wounded deer that retreats from its fellows to a distant glen to lick its Injuries. He repaired often to his office during hours when the doors were normally closed, muttering about "important papers" that had to be completed and filed in the courts on an imminent occasion. He took breakfast uncommonly early and dinner inconveniently late in order to avoid his regular mealtime companions. If he were walking along the side of the road and saw an acquaintance approaching, he would deliberately cross to the other side so as not to become engaged in conversation.

When I described these curious ailments and discombobulations to the President, he rose from his chair, threw up his hands, and laughed uproariously.

"Why Annie-Belle, do you not see the signs as clearly as the dome on the Capitol? The young man is in love!"

"Oh it certainly looks that way, Sir. I do not deny it. Nor was I unaware of the symptoms. But does young Blair know what he is afflicted with?"

"By now, I am certain, though perhaps not yesterday or the day before."

"And why are you so positive?"

By way of answering, Andrew walked over to a nearby bookshelf and picked out a volume, wedged in amongst the law journals and state documents. He held it up so that I could read the title, "Love Poems by Robert Burns."

"He was perusing the pages avidly last evening and earnestly scribbling excerpts on a sheet of foolscap. Does that suggest anything to you?"

Any doubts I might have had fluttered away like moths during the next few days. Truxton's actions were out of character, to say the least. He was seen on several occasions totally immersed in one or another volume of poetry --

instead of poring over law journals and Congressional papers. He evidenced a sudden Interest in nature and the flora and fauna of the woodlands -- setting aside his usual inquiries into the occurrences at various courts of law. He was thoughtful enough one afternoon to bring home a fanciful arrangement of flowers for the dinner table -- whereas in the past he was wont to look upon mealtimes as intrusions on one's time, rather than pleasant interludes for refreshing body and soul.

The President noticed the metamorphosis even more than I did and reacted with consummate enjoyment. For some months, he had been encouraging Truxton to visit him in his study two or three evenings a week for as much as an hour. Not only did he find these discussions provocative and stimulating, but he welcomed the opportunity to learn how young people in Washington viewed the issues of the day. Truxton had been an excellent sounding board.

But after the riding accident in late November, Andrew noticed -- and not without relish! -- a marked change in the nature of the topics his young protégé seemed inclined to discuss.

"I did not know before now that the lad had any sentience for homely affairs like architecture or furniture or fabrics," he said to me with a meaningful look and a twinkle in his eye, "yet his thoughts seem to be in that direction."

"Would you say, Sir, to borrow an expression from nature, that he is hoping to feather a nest?"

"Most assuredly. Only yesterday, he inquired whether I knew of any good land available within easy riding distance of the capital, where a small homestead might readily be constructed."

"Are you thinking of moving out of the White House?

"Oh, no, Sir, no." His face was a-fluster and he gave a nervous laugh, "but I should be thinking about an investment in land now. For the future."

"I agreed heartily and gave him the name of a freeholder in Arlington whom I know to be honest and who has more acreage than he can manage.

Symptoms of a man afflicted with that most happy delirium: love. Yet I did not realize how deeply Truxton's emotions flowed until I discovered a remarkable fact. Somehow, using his increasingly glib tongue, he had induced Andrew into discussing the one subject he had long concealed within his breast: *Rachel*. The President had inner feelings so strong at this time, one year after her death that he kept them locked inside. Oh, they revealed their presence from time to time, largely in the way he reacted to the personal tragedies of other widowers or widows, and his preoccupation with young people in love. But the President almost never permitted Rachel's name to be drawn into a conversation.

Why did he break his principle?

For one thing, since he saw in Becky the image of Rachel and in Truxton so much an image of his own younger self, he did not mind opening his heart. Equally persuasive was the probability that he needed to relieve the pressure of long silence and acknowledge the real extent of his grief.

Becky remained, as ever, close to the President and much in his thoughts, though she did not share in any conversations about Rachel. It was evident to Andrew -- and to all of us within the Presidential circle -- that she was in love.

She moved with that lightness of body characteristic of a disciple of Aphrodite. Her countenance reflected the vacillations of mood so common to lovers: intoxicated with faith one moment, engulfed by doubt the next.

Her mode of dress underwent a transformation that I found most amusing. Shunning the frontier look and the vigorous styling of her dark tresses, she took to wearing lacy frocks with diaphanous over-shawls. She replaced her deerskin riding boots with velvet pumps. In short, she modified her wardrobe to relate to the drawing room instead of the fields and the woodlands.

Regularly, too, she could be found of an evening seated in the library with her book of grammar or in the writing alcove practicing her penmanship.

The reason for these innovations was most transparent, at least to the rest of us: she wanted to reshape her primeval image (*gloriously becoming though it was to her!*) into that of the more civilized and sophisticated lady of the manor that Truxton seemed to place on his personal pedestal.

Though I had moments of anguish, fearing that her vivacious and dynamic personality might become as saccharine as her fashion, I need not have worried. Her nature was as peppery as ever -- perhaps a little more so, spiced by the strength of her passion.

She was suddenly aware of the immensity of Truxton's emotional reservoir and his capacity for loving. She had no intention of letting him dam it all up behind a wall of dispassion and constraint, excused by a sudden surge of "dedication" to his firm and his career.

Pretentiousness was an acquired, not a natural trait. If Truxton appeared too pompous at times, it was no more a real part of him than the wig he wore on solemn, legislative occasions. Becky was determined to disrobe this image as quickly and manifestly as possible.

I had the fortune (whether good or bad) to play the part of the lady bug on the lintel, one Sunday afternoon. Sitting in the small enclosed veranda off the West Wing of the White House, I heard Becky and Truxton approaching along the adjoining corridor. Hidden from view by a clump of potted boxthorn, I was about to stand up and speak to them when I realized that Becky was furious. My best strategy was to remain silent and hope they would pass on by, never noticing me at all.

"Oh! Oh! I should douse your face in icy well water," she chided, "until it makes some blood race across your cheeks. You act like a stuffed puppet, filled with sawdust and sponge."

She did not spare a few reproofs in a saltier idiom. It did my heart good to know that, although she was attired in the vogue of the parlour, her language bespoke the vigor of the frontier. I wish that I could have seen as well as heard. Truxton's countenance must have been magnificent to behold, with eyes agape, tongue sputtering, and face starting to flush like poppies.

I knew that his lips were as dry as flour, for I heard him try to respond in his usual well coordinated, well modulated tones. Instead, his voice cracked -- the same voice that had convinced obdurate judges of the certitude of his clients' claims or that had flabbergasted fledgling Congressmen who were intent on denouncing the President's party.

Young Blair did not choke up for long. He was too strong-spirited and too responsive to the girl's vibrant, yet affectionate, language. His own emotions came pouring out in a manner reminiscent of his boyhood in Tennessee, when I knew him as a kind of unbridled colt, not always appreciated by his father, the Colonel, who had been schooled in the military convention.

The crackle of their conversation mellowed somewhat as they proceeded down the corridor, their voices finally fading completely. I pictured Becky taking his arm gently and composing herself back into parlour gentility as they approached the stairwell leading up to the first floor where, like as not, they would encounter some of their peers, if not the President himself.

The relationship between Becky and Truxton grew closer and less tempestuous as the weeks past. By the time we saw the New Year in and wondered what 1830 would bring, they were thought of as lovers and close to the time when they would officially announce their engagement. The White House was an ideal place for love to flourish, offering more than the usual share of places for trysts. There were all kinds of passageways and alcoves, chimney corners and dens, anterooms and secret stairways.

Outside, when the weather was clement, two people in love could be alone and undisturbed in dozens of groves, woodland paths, summer houses, arboreta, horse sheds, and outbuildings. Horseback rides of less than half an hour would take them to forest glens and hidden streams not much changed from their wilderness stages hundreds of years ago.

Even when Truxton became increasingly involved in political affairs and had to spend late hours at the Capitol, Becky would gallop down in the dusk to meet him, if only for a brief tryst. There were any number of unoccupied rooms, some still housing workmen's augurs and bits and saws as work on the building continued at a laborious pace.

Often they met with friends in the Sacristy of the South Capital Church to plan the next step in their fund-raising campaign for the Alexandria orphanage. There they would linger, after the others had departed, for quiet moments together before mounting their horses and cantering back to the White House.

Vicariously, I relished every minute of their love affair. I relived my own amorous adventures of the past. Oh, perhaps I did indulge a bit too much in imaginative fantasies. If I happened to spot them out in the garden of an evening, locked in each other's arms, I could not help picturing how vigorously they would make love in bed. If I saw them sitting before the fire caressing each other gently before parting to go to their separate chambers, I would tingle all over as my mind was flooded with sensuous memories of my own interludes of ecstasy.

I knew that Andrew, in his own way, saw the emotional reflections of his courtship of Rachel four decades earlier. He neither pried nor questioned them about their intentions. Yet he could not help noticing many of the little sings of love: the way they looked at each other at the dinner table, the brushing of fingertips across the back of a hand, the gentle modulations of voice, the touch of lips on meeting or parting.

Throughout that winter, Andrew and I had numerous conversations about love and the Young in Heart, most of the chats being casual and brief. What surprised me most was that he occasionally mentioned Rachel, both in a matter-of-fact way and with emotion. He almost never before had allowed her name to creep into any conversation, even when talking with his most intimate friends.

"You know," he mused one day, almost as though he were thinking out loud to himself, "Becky and Truxton have a few obstacles to overcome. Yet they are largely matters of outlook and personality, not uncommon to young people in love. Thank God, they are not plagued by the prodigious legal disputes that Rachel and I faced. We were in a maelstrom so great during our courtship, and after our first marriage, that we would never have embarked on our romance had we guessed what lay ahead."

Discussions about the Young in Heart were like tonic to Andrew. I had not seen him in such fresh spirits and staunch fettle for months.

By mid-March, after a damp, chilly winter, signs of spring began to emerge. A perfect time of year for lovers. And for all young people. What a shame it was that now, having reached a pleasant pinnacle in his personal life and when he was finally coping with the tragic death of Rachel, he should face rebuke for his compassion. Prying into his exuberant commitment to his extensive White House family, his enemies were already plotting ways to unseat him, or at least seriously dissipate his Presidential powers. Henry Clay, ever the busybody, was coining derogatory phrases that he felt would tarnish the President's image.

"Mr. Jackson is a coddler. He pampers those who dwell in his palace on Pennsylvania Avenue while he lets the rest of us go to the Devil! Our relationships with Mexico deteriorate in the West while he sips tea with young maidens in the East Portico. He ignores the fact that our Army needs guns while he arms his little bow with an arrow so that he may play the part of Cupid."

And so it continued. We were to learn how brutal his enemies could be. But first, we were -- all of us at the White House -- to be shocked by unexpected tragedy and left bereaved and unnerved.

Chapter 12

The weather was sunny but windy that late Sunday afternoon in March, 1830. I had gone from my lodgings to the White House to pick up some corn cakes that the pastry cook had saved for me. Just as I entered the kitchen, redolent with the fragrance of hickory wood smoke and the odor of a roast of beef in the oven, one of the servant boys came running in from the rear garden path.

"Accident, accident," he cried breathlessly, barely able to speak after the exertions of a long, fast run."

"What kind of accident?" I asked with alarm.

"Person been drowned. Drowned dead. Down at the Potomac.

When the cook and I calmed him down enough so his words made sense, my alarm was even greater. According to his report, one of the "White House young misses" had been lost when a small boat capsized.

"Oh, it cannot be, it cannot be," moaned the cook, telling me that six or seven young people had mounted horses and headed towards the river shortly after lunch. I knew exactly where a small dock was located, belonging to the White House. Tied to it would be several rowboats, a wherry and a lapstrake sailing skiff.

From the boy's description -- he had seen the victim pulled from beneath the water and placed on the river bank --the first image that came to my mind was that of Becky Hayes.

Fate could not be that cruel! Not after all that had transpired in the unfortunate girl's life and she had finally found happiness within her grasp.

I rushed outside to the rail, untied my horse, and galloped the half mile or so to the boat house and dock. Two rivermen were by the shore, pulling the skiff onto the beach. Almost before they told me, I could see from the look of shock on their faces that there had indeed been a tragedy.

"Don't know ta name of a young miss," said the older of the two, "a pretty, pretty lass. A took her yonder to Army's infirmary." He shook his head sadly, "Aye, a pretty, pretty miss."

"There was a doctor here, then?" For a moment I felt a flush of hope.

"No, Ma'm. Twaren't. Only a musketman. He and a young lad what were in ta boat slung the poor miss over a bale of straw and tried to pound the water outen her lungs. Then they hastened her to ta infirmary."

"A young lad ? Was he tow-headed?"

"Couldna say, Ma'm. Sorry. His hair was so wet."

He pointed out the infirmary, a mile or so downstream and three or four hundred yards east of the Potomac. I galloped off.

The first person I saw there was Sam Hays, standing by the doorway, sodden wet, head in hands, and weeping profusely. He was clearly in a state of shock.

"Who. . .?" I began.

"Flora. Flora!" he blurted in a broken voice, without waiting for my question. "She's gone. Gone!"

Flora Hutchinson. My heart was broken. I went inside and was informed by the doctor that her body lay in a back room and that there was no hope. My poor, dear child had been under the water too long.

With great difficulty, I pried the details from Cora Livingstone, who was huddled under a drab army blanket, shivering more from hysteria than from the cold. She, Flora, Peggy, and Sam had put out from shore in the lapstrake skiff. After raising the sail, small though it was, they had been caught in a squall and upset.

Sam had urged all of the girls to cling to the boat. Cora and Peggy had heeded his advice but Flora, who was adept at a new method of swimming called the sidestroke, had removed her boots and set out for shore. In no time, she was floundering under the weight of her clothing.

Seeing her distress, Sam had torn off all of his own clothes save his knickers and flailed the water in pursuit. Though he was an able swimmer himself, he could not move quickly enough. Flora sank beneath the churning, muddy waters barely 100 feet from the boathouse. The rivermen had waded out to assist, but could go only so far, having no knowledge at all of how to keep afloat.

Sam dove and dove for our pretty child, but by the time he had managed to clutch her dress and haul her to dry land, her lungs had filled with water. Rolling her over the bale of straw and pounding her back dislodged but a small proportion of the deadly liquid that was choking the life from her. Their final hope was to get her immediately into the hands of a physician. But alas it was too late.

I was struck with a terrifying thought. Where was Andrew Jackson? How would he react to this tragedy?

My recollection was that he had intended to go to the Capitol for a Sunday afternoon meeting with Mr. Calhoun and Mr. Van Buren to review the military budget. As it turned out, he was even at that moment riding back towards the White House when he was intercepted by a courier on horseback who reigned up alongside and informed him that there had been an accident.

For two days the President was paralyzed with grief. He remained, almost incommunicado, in his chambers until emerging for the funeral, at which he delivered a moving eulogy. It was several more days before he lifted himself out of his somber mood and was able to shake off the horror of that afternoon.

"You would not believe that a person my age is susceptible to nightmares," he confessed to me, "but the spectre of death has visited me in my sleep. I have winced to see his evil face and beady eyes as he carried off that lovely, irreplaceable child in the flower of youth.

"Ahh, Annie-Belle, would that the Spectre had seized me instead of Flora! But I am sure he would have found me too sparse and bony for his taste."

By the time he had completely dispelled his morbid humours we were into the middle of April. The prospect of spring and new life all around cheered him greatly. Death was no longer in the air, but a vicious malignancy was breeding. Political enemies were scheming underhanded ways of discrediting the President and weakening his power.

Such a campaign challenged their ingenuity for Andrew was (in my opinion) as solidly entrenched in his office as a tortoise is in his shell. He had been receiving fine encomiums from editors, one of whom wrote in the

Washington <u>Intelligencer</u> that "Mr. Jackson's popularity can withstand *anything.*"

Another pointed out that, whatever flaws the President had, they did not include vacillation, untrustworthiness, or disloyalty and that "he stands by those that stood by him, rockbound."

Some of his earlier detractors who had predicted that he would come to Washington "little advanced in civilization over the Indians with whom he made war" were now swallowing their opinions. One such journalist wrote of him as being gracious, reserved, and "more presidential in bearing than any of the other candidates."

With this kind of strength blocking their efforts, his personal enemies and political adversaries despaired of ever tarnishing his public image. Still, a few old-line bulldogs like Henry Clay persisted, always looking for vulnerable points of attack. It was Clay himself who pointed out that, although Jackson was as impregnable as the bastion of a fort, there were always rear entrances that could be breached. By this he meant that some of those associated with the President might be vulnerable.

He singled out Truxton Blair, who was prone to expressing himself or acting in dissenting, nonconformist ways that could be attacked and criticized much more effectively than conventional approaches. Clay was a friend of the editor of the <u>Intelligencer</u>, the Capital's major newspaper, and was thus able to plant certain stories and seed rumors about Blair. Yet even Clay was continuously being frustrated when young Blair's schemes drew unexpected public support.

I recall well the incident at the Capitol in mid-spring...

Mr. William Duane, Secretary of the Treasury -- whom I considered a most stuffy individual -- all but barged into the President' office in a state of consternation.

"You will scarcely believe, Mr. President, what that reckless young Blair has been up to..."

"To the contrary, I can believe almost anything," interrupted Andrew with a laugh that seemed to surge all the way up from his stomach, "and anything he has concocted that arouses indignation is probably something I shall cherish, let alone condone. He is my spirit reincarnate you know, so be judicious in your choice of verbal recriminations."

"Well, umph," faltered this dignitary, not certain how to proceed, "he has gone so far as to throw his gauntlet on the Senate floor."

"You mean he has challenged one of the senators to a *duel*?"

"Not quite such an atrocious act, Sir. But almost. As you may know, he has openly expressed opposition to re-chartering the Bank of the United States."

"A position I firmly endorse.

"True. True. But Blair has had the temerity to have a copy of the Charter laboriously written in ink by a public scribe, but in a most enlarged hand -- six or eight times what it might be on a legal document."

"Go on, go on, Dear Sir, you have aroused my interest and curiosity unquenchably."

"Well, Mr. President, having made this bank charter, or the beginnings of it, into a poster, he marched around the perimeter of the Capitol until he had collected a large crowd of passers-by. Then he positioned himself right where most of the construction workers are at their busiest, trying to complete the Bullfinch arch.

"Ahhh, yes, he *would* do that. Quite a tribute to bureaucratic bungling there, littered with splintered timbers and misshapen blocks of granite, and a sea of shavings and dust."

"Yes. Yes. Most unfortunate to be able to see why the nation's architecture is behind schedule. At any rate Blair now unveiled a second poster showing a caricature of the Bank of the United States. Its facade was distorted so the columns looked like rows of teeth -- all chewing up American currency.

"This is what will happen to our money!" he informed the crowd repeatedly, "if we re-charter the Bank."

Chapter 13

Andrew Jackson *was* a firm believer in the Devil.

"Satan is a necessary evil," he used to tell me, long before he ever ran for the Presidency, "to goad mankind into undertaking steps to change history. New nations must be born in hellfire, as America was; sired by Satan, as the republic was; tested in the heat of anarchy and rebellion, as our Constitution was; fibered to be cantankerous and perverse in infancy, as our population now is -- to stand up to those who would do the Devil's work, but to their own self-interest."

He spoke to me of "swords and shot and shell for the republic, forged in the fires of hell" and "the very iron of the nation's backbone tempered in the glowing coals, tended by demons."

I had long forgotten his fiery expositions on the birth of our nation, harking back to the days in 1796 when Tennessee was being taken into the Union and undergoing some "tempering" of her own.

Now I was about to meet the devil in a more familiar guise.

I had driven over to the White House in my surrey to pick up Cora Livingstone. We were to dine at a French bistro that had opened near the Mall, underwritten by two members of the French delegation who pined for authentic Gallic cuisine. I had not expected to see the President at all. But just as I stepped down at the hitching post, he came storming out the great portal door, evidently having expected me to be some one else.

It was plain to see that he was furious. The telltale scar across his forehead was glowing and throbbing like flickering coals.

"That Clay, that blackheart, this time he has gone too far. I shall yet see my sword in his guts!"

"Whatever is the matter, Mr. President?" I asked, face calm but heart thumping inside me as it did during such outbursts of raw emotion.

"Henry Clay -- that's what's the matter! He is the Devil incarnate."

When he saw who I was, he composed himself at once.

I offered him my hand and he pushed down the white cuff of the glove to kiss my wrist in his usual fervent manner.

"Come in, come in, Annie-Belle. How would you like to help me take this cane to those who find pleasure in bedeviling me?"

He raised his ever-present hickory walking stick high in the air. For a moment I thought he was going to smash it against one of the newly painted pilasters. We went inside and sat down in the East tea chamber.

Without waiting for my answer, he continued heatedly, "If Clay wants to play the curmudgeon, I'll show him how this old ram can butt back."

Clay was a statesman, a man of stature and influence, and a figure who would surely leave his mark on American history. I could not deny that, nor could Andrew (*though he would never admit such a profane thought.*) But the man was sly and self-centered and never the one to let an opportunity slip if he could cut down an opponent or inflict verbal lashes where they would smart the most.

"All this fiddle ..." Now, explained the President testily and impatiently, Clay had been guilty of one of the worst political sins: invading the intimate, private life of a public figure. "He has charged that I, the President, have been turning the White House into an *orphanage*. And to such a degree that I have neglected the most pressing concerns of our nation!"

"Pooh! He is jealous, Sir, that you are surrounded by the Young in Heart. He has eleven offspring. Tell him to bring them to Washington, where they might serve their country better than as housemaids and stable boys on his stagnant Kentucky plantation.

"He is an intense busybody," continued Andrew bitterly after a potion of gin and water had somewhat assuaged the turbulence within him, "I don't know how he ever found out about young Blair and Mistress Becky ...

Becky? Truxton?

Had something occurred that I did not know about? Was there trouble? A secret marriage? An unwanted pregnancy? My heart fluttered.

"What on earth does Henry Clay have to do with our two handsome lovers?"

"The less, the better!" he grumped, "It isn't them actually what's the target, but *me*. He has poked his long, sniffling nose right into this house. Now he has gone back and announced to Congress -- like some Tory spy! -- that I am in my dotage, neglecting my executive duties, and pouring all my time and energies into playing Cupid."

Suddenly he threw up his long, twiggy arms and laughed raucously, "well, of course I have been playing Cupid. But it's none of his Goddamned business that I have a heart for young people and their affairs."

"Henry is *supposed* to be a Man of the People. Why then has he not yet learned that the republic, in order to survive and bloom, must be nurtured by love?

"Love. Oh, not the conventional affection and understanding, leader to leader or husband to wife, but love in the vigorous sense, with all the emotion and outpourings and the sensuality and sensitivities of romance. What does a nation thrive on in the end if not young lovers with all their impetuosity and heat and naiveté, the roiling juices of passion and the steaming emotions and the ferment.

"That's what America needs. And that, by God, is what America shall have -- Henry Clay or no!"

The President paused abruptly and cupped the shagbark skin of his hollow cheeks in his long, bony fingers and closed his eyes.

I said nothing and remained motionless.

For perhaps three minutes Andrew hunched that way, almost as though in a trance. I knew that he was reliving a youthful episode with his own beloved Rachel, just as realistically and fervently as though she had been brought back from the dead and granted a brief span of resurrection. It was easy for me to picture them -- a passionate young man and an amorous sweetheart -- in each other's arms. Or strolling as one along the mossy banks of the Cumberland. Or riding the trails.

Just as abruptly as he had lost himself in his memories, the President shook himself and snapped erect, eyeing me with momentary surprise. Then he returned quickly to his former trend of conversation.

"Is he a President or a Cupid running around naked with his little bow and arrow?" That's what Clay asked, rhetorically, in public. Andrew threw back his head so hard that even his stiff, broomstick hair quivered. "Not satisfied with trying to make me look the jackass, he called my interest in my family a 'fatal diversion.' Well, I must not dwell on these matters. I have too much to accomplish, Annie-Belle, and I must get on with things."

I did not see the President again for several weeks, for he was engaged in travels to Philadelphia and New York. It was fortunate that he was away from the White House at this time, for Becky Hays and Truxton Blair were experiencing a tempest in their love affair. The situation was not at first cause for alarm, since both lovers were temperamental and Truxton at times volatile. Yet their lovers' quarrels would have most certainly distracted the President -- and at a time when he was pressed on all sides with executive problems.

"You are very hateful, Mr. Blair, and I hope that you shan't be intruding on my affairs any longer."

I overheard Becky voicing several such opinions to her betrothed, with increasing impatience and excitability. What was going wrong? It was Rebecca McLane (*who herself had a characteristic Irish temper*) who finally shed light on the cause. Becky had impetuously agreed to head up the local fund-raising campaign for the orphanage at Alexandria. Though it was a cause we all believed in, there had been some confusion about the goals of the institution. Truxton had strong opposed Becky's increased involvement, especially since he was trying to button down the plans for their own future.

"I look forward to sitting down of an evening with Becky," he complained one day, "and discussing a few questions -- and where is she ? Down at Alexandria conferring with an architect. Or over at Arlington trying to raise money from a church. Or maybe down at the Mall passing around a hat. I am fast losing patience with her."

"But it is an important cause, Truxton," Becky would try to explain again and again, "Do you not, as an orphan yourself, have sympathy for other orphans who might not be so fortunate as to be invited to live at the White House."

"Sympathy, yes. But this Alexandria project is said to have some exalted goal of which I am not aware. If it is more noble than that of all the other orphanages in the country, people must surely want to know before they donate anything more than a handful of copper."

"That is true," acknowledged Becky, "but we have an unusual plan -- even the President himself is working out the final details

"Mr. Jackson? But you cannot count on him. He has a hundred pressing issues that require his attention. He does not have time. Besides, you are nearing your deadline and you cannot wait until the President sets aside important matters to resolve a charity drive.

"Charity drive!" Becky fumed at this implication by Truxton -- just one of several -- that her dedicated labors were of minor consequence. The gulf between the two lovers widened so seriously that on one occasion Becky plucked the engagement ring from her finger and threw it at her fiancé.

When Andrew Jackson returned to the White House that spring after his tour of the Northeast, I saw little of him. He was indeed under pressure from all sides. Moreover, I was fearfully aware that his political enemies were massing forces. It would soon be time to launch campaign plans for the election of 1832. Henry Clay had already tried one stratagem: to instigate a vote of censure against Jackson by the Senate. Since he had *almost* succeeded, it was logical that he would try a second time.

To wound the President with an official censure would leave scars that could impede his candidacy.

My greatest worry was that Andrew would, in his characteristic, emotional way become involved in the romantic plight of the two lovers. That would be his undoing, for Clay and his cronies would be quick to see that the President was devoting much time and energy to "personal business," and less to affairs of state. It would do no good for Andrew to use "invasion of privacy" as a counterclaim, a charge that had fended off the brunt of criticism in the past.

The issue came to a head one cloudy day in June, when the air was heavy with threats of a storm outside the Capitol, while inside the great domed structure political opponents were squaring off in several corners. The atmosphere was particularly tense in one council chamber where Henry Clay was haranguing a conference of twelve senators seated around an oval walnut table.

"In the West," he proclaimed in somber tones, "we have Mexico disputing our boundary claims. But where is Mr. Jackson? I have not seen him for three days.

"To the North, we have the threat of Indians plundering villages in New Hampshire and Vermont. But where is the President?

"Abroad, we have the French refusing to pay for damages to American ships during the Napoleonic Wars. Is Mr. Jackson here to add insistence to our voices of protest?

"Right here in Washington, we are stumbling in our efforts to complete building projects necessary for the very administration of our government. But where is our President?

"I shall tell you. For at least half of this week, he has secluded himself at the White House where he amuses himself by running a congenial boarding house for young pea-pie and acting as arbitrator in solving lovers' quarrels.

I tell you, gentlemen, as a former cabinet member and as an advisor to this council, you must draft and deliver to the Senate an official censure to be put to the vote."

"Aye, aye." Many were the voices of approval and many the affirmative shaking of heads, even from several senators who had steadfastly remained supporters of Andrew Jackson in the past.

But the Devil himself was abroad that stormy day.

All at once there was a bustle in the hall and the sound of heavy footsteps on the polished hardwood floor. The heavy walnut door swung open and in strode Andrew Jackson, as unexpected as though he had been the Creator in person.

Was it pure chance that he had selected this chamber? Or did he have some mystical intimation that forces were concentrated here that meant him no good? No one will ever know. My own theory is that he sniffed out Henry Clay, perceiving that wherever Clay's boots stood, mischief would be right underfoot.

The staid members of the council looked up, consternation flickering on their faces. Clay's jowls drooped, though he quickly recovered his composure and masked his dismay with his characteristically genial smile. Despite the presence of the enemy at the doorstep he could yet carry out his planned strategy. Of a sudden he was struck with an inspiration. Why not tell the President that they have missed his presence at the Capitol this critical week and express the hope that he has been enjoying his leisure at the White House?

He was about to speak, as they all rose in respect for the office of President, if not all for the incumbent. But Andrew Jackson waved them to their seats and stood before them, hands locked in his leather vest.

"I am delighted to see the members of this council in session," he began, with a sweeping bow to the silent assemblage, "for I have an announcement of some import to make to you."

None could have been more vexed than Mr. Clay when the President explained that he had passed the last four days in Alexandria "working night and day with some of the most dedicated of our citizens" to secure the final pledges of financial support for the orphanage at Alexandria.

His oratory, reserved usually for issues of great national gravity, was as eloquent as though he were defending the

Constitution itself. The institution was to be unique, not just a shelter for homeless waifs from the Washington and Virginia region, but one of significance in the strength of the republic.

"It will open its doors to selected young people from across our nation who, though left without father or mother to guide them, have shown through scholarship and dedication that they have qualities of leadership.

"The orphanage will be consecrated to those without families who, instead of being lost in the turbulence of uncaring societies, will have a chance to become touched by greatness. Through our efforts, these lost children can be inspired to eminence, dignity, and nobility so that one day they will be the ones who can take the reins from us, with pride and devotion.

"As you know," explained the President, his voice low and breaking just a bit, "I was orphaned at the age of fourteen and left penniless, with little schooling and no close relatives. I might have become a tramp and a drifter had it not been for a combination of luck and a few adults who cared."

He seemed about to end his oration, then laughed heartily and glanced around the room, "Oh, fine Sirs, I am sure there are several of you here who would like to curse those adults for having encouraged those ambitions that eventually led me to Washington! But that is a different log in the fire."

The twelve senators arose and applauded, hardly recalling that not many minutes earlier they had been ready to draft a proposal of censure against this very person. As for Mr. Clay, he clapped weakly, trying to shrink into the background and away from the President's view.

As lovers have been doing for centuries, Becky Hays and Truxton Blair forgot their quarrels and fell into each other's arms again with, if possible, increased ardor and rapture. Early that fall they were married in a modest ceremony in the East Room of the White House, attended only by relatives and friends, as well as the rest of the Young in Heart.

Andrew gave the bride away.

He looked taller, younger, and livelier than he had since the day he was inaugurated!

I was still in love with Andrew Jackson. I guessed I always would be.

THE END